SUGAR TIME

Credits
Design: Methodologie
Author Photo: Emma Lewisohn

10 Digit ISBN: 1-4392-3761-1
13 Digit EAN: 9781439237618

Library of Congress Control Number: 200990372

SUGAR TIME

A NOVEL BY
JANE ADAMS

BY JANE ADAMS

NOVELS

Tradeoffs

Good Intentions

Seattle Green

NONFICTION

Boundary Issues

When Our Grown Kids Disappoint Us

I'm Still Your Mother

Wake Up, Sleeping Beauty

How to Sell What You Write

Making Good: Conversations with Successful Men

Women on Top

Sex and the Single Parent

PLAYS

The Promised Land

CHAPTER
ONE

I was watching a *Seinfeld* re-run and picking at some leftover kung pao chicken when an octopus curled its tentacles around my midsection and squeezed. I should have thrown this food out two days ago, I thought, and then the octopus squeezed again and took my breath away. Beads of sweat popped out on my forehead and my skin went all damp and clammy. Great. A hot flash and heartburn at the same time. Welcome to modern maturity. That's the time between your first copy of the AARP magazine and your first social security check, when you start getting used to the idea that you're not only not middle aged any longer, you're old. Unless you expect to live forever, of course—which, up to then, you sort of do.

There was a little pink bottle of Pepto-Bismol in a striped ditty bag in the bathroom that I've carted all over the world in case I get sick from eating food from the street, which I never have and always do; my philosophy is, if you're going to play it safe, you might as well stay home. But I couldn't get to it—a wave of torpor held me down on the couch like an invisible force field. After a few minutes the octopus seemed to relent, so I tried moving. But then it snaked itself around my ribcage and let me know it was still there.

The phone rang, but there was no way I could reach it—it was only a couple of feet away but it might as well have been in the apartment next door. It rang seven times before voice mail finally kicked in; I counted them while I tried to remember how long ago I'd ordered in that chicken.

Maybe it wasn't food poisoning; it might be a kidney stone. I've never had one, but once on a flight from L.A. the man in the aisle seat told me in excruciating detail how he'd once passed one on the seventeenth green. Actually, I don't remember whether it was a kidney stone or a gallstone, only that when the stewardess held out the little cup of olives for his martini, the way they used to in first class, he'd just gotten to the part about how he still managed to finish the round a respectable three over par. He didn't say that passing a stone felt like a contraction that went on and on, although to be fair, he couldn't have known that. But he also didn't seem the type who'd asked his wife how it really felt to birth little Tiger Woods Junior, either.

I took shallow, silent little breaths so the octopus wouldn't notice, and let go of the remote; for some reason I'd muted the TV when the octopus struck, and when the phone stopped ringing it was suddenly unnaturally silent in the room. I felt alone and abandoned, like I'd fallen overboard without anyone on deck noticing while the boat disappeared over the horizon; when I turned the volume on again my arm tingled the way your foot does when you try to move it after it's fallen asleep, and then the tingle heated up a couple of hundred degrees and radiated in waves down to my fingers.

"Oh shit," I said out loud, "I'm having a heart attack!"

Tory looked up from her pillow—not hearing any magic words like 'Let's go out,' or 'Do you want a treat?' she went right back to doggy dreamland. It was beginning to dawn on me that if I didn't do something, call someone, get myself moving, I was going to die right here, all by myself, on a faded green velvet sofa surrounded by greasy white cardboard containers, a half empty can of Diet Coke, and the latest issue of Vanity Fair. Shuffle off this mortal coil in my ratty old sweats, irony of ironies, to the theme song from *Going It Alone*, which follows *Seinfeld* on weeknights on *Nick at Nite*. Live by TV, die by it, I used to say. *But please, God, I didn't really mean it.*

I managed to drag the phone over, but then I couldn't decide who to call. Ignoring the mocking voice in my head—*Help, you've fallen and you can't get up, call 911, what are you waiting for?*—I pushed "6"on the speed dial instead. I'd rather be dead than carted through the lobby on a gurney under the rheumy gaze of Mrs. Bosenberg, who lives in One A and keeps an eye on the lobby, just in case Louie the night doorman is sleeping on the job.

Mrs. B.'s apartment is rent-stabilized, which means they can't throw her out. So is mine, and the only way anyone ever leaves a rent stabilized apartment in New York, especially a classic five on the upper West Side, is feet first. After the relatives of the deceased have finished sitting *shiva*, the owners haul away all the dark, heavy furniture and slap on a few coats of paint and then they put the place on the market for a sum that could foment a revolution in an African backwater. Since nobody was doing that to my stuff, especially not until I took my vibrator out from under the bed, cleaned out my stash of recreational drugs, and threw away some pictures I'd just as soon nobody saw, I'd rather let Mrs. B. think I was catching the red-eye to the coast.

I'd managed to hold onto the apartment even after I moved to L.A. Every month when I sent the management company the rent, which was less than people pay their gardeners out there, I thought of it as a hedge against having to grow old in a place where women over 21 are invisible unless they're very powerful, and even then they have to file an environmental impact study before going out in public.

I slid my feet into a pair of well-worn Tod's and pulled an old suede jacket around me, clutching it tightly while the octopus let up enough for me to inch my way to the elevator in slow, clumsy steps. By the time the doors opened downstairs in the lobby, though, it was back, and this time it was really pissed off.

Getting to the front door seemed to take forever. I was glad Louie was off getting stoned in the basement with his brother-in-law the super instead of guarding the door. One look at me and he'd be calling the real estate brokers to tell them there was a vacancy coming up in the building.

The gray Lincoln town car was already waiting at the curb. Somehow I managed to get into the back seat without collapsing on the sidewalk. The driver didn't even turn around.

"Where to?" he asked.

As a rule, your better Manhattan hospitals are on the east side, but since Roosevelt-St. Luke's was the closest that's where I told him to take me. "The emergency room entrance," I added.

I wasn't hurting so much and I was breathing a little easier so I called Teddy from the car. He's a gay actor who lives on my block and has a key to my apartment in case I'm tied up and can't get home to feed and water Tory. I left him a message asking him to take care of her until I called him and then we were at the hospital. The driver leaned over me and opened the door; an orderly who'd been catching a surreptitious toke a few feet from the entrance pinched off the tip of his joint and pocketed it before he looked me over, said "Right back," and returned a few seconds later with a wheelchair, still trailing the punky odor of dope.

After that it's mostly blank. I think I passed out somewhere between "Do you have an insurance card?" and "What seems to be the problem?" because the next thing I remember was blinking away the bright light that was shining in my eyes.

A youngish, balding guy in wire-rimmed glasses and green pajamas bent over me.

"Dr. Greene, good to see you again." My voice sounded in my ears as if it was coming from a long way away. "I was really sorry when you got that brain tumor and died." And then my eyes closed again and they stayed that way until some time later—fifteen minutes, an hour?—when I woke up with a tube in my nose, an IV in my arm and a bitter taste in my mouth.

The bald guy was back. Or maybe he'd never left. "Do you know where you are?" he asked.

Miraculously, it seemed, the pain had retreated. I took a deep breath of heavily processed air—not nitrous, unfortunately, just plain old oxygen, but I was grateful nonetheless. "County General? Seattle Grace? St. Elsewhere?" If my head wasn't so fuzzy, I could have reeled off a few more. But I could tell he wasn't sure if I was kidding or hallucinating.

"You're at Roosevelt-St. Luke's. I'm Dr. O'Neill, the attending cardiologist."

"O'Neill? What kind of name is that for a cardiologist? Get me a Bernstein or a Goldberg." I can't help it—when I'm nervous or scared, I resort to shtick. Okay, even when I'm *not* nervous and scared. When you don't know what else to say, shtick gets you by until you can come up with something better. Not that there *is* anything better most of the time, at least in my estimation. But what else would you expect from the girl voted "Class Clown" in high school?

"Sorry, but I'm taking their calls tonight," he said.

Now I wasn't sure whether he was kidding.

"I guess it wasn't the kung pao chicken, was it?"

"Not unless you eat it all the time."

"Not all the time. Sometimes I have sweet and sour spareribs or hoisin lamb."

"We're going to have to do something about that," he said, frowning.

Sure, let's sue Empire Szechuan. I could almost hear my ex-husband suggesting it. That's what he does. Like Pavarotti sings and Barry Bonds bats, Ted sues. It wasn't always like that. When I met him, he was a struggling Legal Aid lawyer. Now the only thing he fights is tort reform.

"Did I have a..." I couldn't say it. "What happened?"

"That's not entirely clear. We're not ruling anything out yet. We're waiting on some blood work. Your ECG is a little spiky, but you responded to the nitro, which is good. It might just be angina. Or maybe a little heart attack. Think of it as a wake-up call. A warning."

Some warning. Usually all it takes for me to give up Chinese food is not being able to zip up my jeans.

"We'll know more in a little while," O'Neill said. "We're going to monitor you pretty closely for the next 24 hours. Is there someone one you'd like us to contact—a family member?"

I shook my head.

"Really? How about a friend or neighbor?"

"No," I said. "Don't call anyone." Twenty-four hours I could deal with. Any longer than that and I'd have to think about what I was going to tell the people who really needed to know. Once I figured out who they were, that is.

When Jessie went to South America to study weaving or learn Spanish or whatever it was that convinced me to say yes, I made her promise never to have anyone call me from a hospital and ask if I was her mother.

"Why not?" she wanted to know.

"I'd fall apart if that happened."

"You're right—I'll tell them not to call 'till I'm dead."

"Bite your tongue. Just don't even tell me you were there until later. Much later. Never would be fine, too. Or when you're completely okay."

"But what if I'm not?" She was stubborn, my kid.

"Then tell me when you are."

"How can I if I'm dead or unconscious?"

"You won't be. You'll be fine." Thus do mothers beseech the universe, taking it on faith that someone is listening—if you couldn't, you'd never let them out of your sight.

No, I didn't want the doctor to call Jessie. Especially since she was pregnant. Besides, it didn't look like there was any need to worry her. A warning, he said. That's all. Just a warning.

"How much longer am I going to be here?" I asked.

"We'll know more tomorrow."

"Then I'll call someone tomorrow."

CHAPTER
TWO

The rhythmic whooshing noise might have been train wheels that were somehow connected to the last fragment of a dream that dissipated when I woke up. I could tell it was morning by the thin gray light creeping in through the vertical window shades; my watch was gone, replaced by a white plastic bracelet with my name on it.

"Doctor will be glad to see you're awake. He's been in twice already." A heavy-set black woman with a white starched pancake on her head was doing something to a plastic clothespin that was clamped to my middle finger and attached to the machine responsible for that whooshing sound. Every few seconds it emitted a little beep, like a smoke detector with a failing battery.

"What time is it? Can I get some coffee? Do I really need to be hooked up to that thing?"

"Until Doctor says it's okay and we move you out of the CCU," She pronounced "Doctor" so reverently she might have been talking about God; in my estimation, only English novelists should be allowed to use a job description like a proper noun. "Until then, we need to keep an eye on your numbers," she added.

Is that what I'd been reduced to, I wondered—numbers? What about the actual person, the human being in this bed who's dying for a cup of coffee and needs to pee in the worst way—what about her? What can a bunch of numbers tell you about Sugar Kane, an accomplished, even a successful woman, a great broad, a funny dame, yes, a woman of a certain age, (which sounds so much sexier and more mysterious, if somewhat less specific in French, which is the point, right?) but still, somebody's mother, somebody's daughter, somebody's lover…. well, not currently, maybe, but that's not the point: What happened to Sugar nee Charlotte Sugarman, who became Sugar Kane when she married her college boyfriend because she couldn't convince him to change it back to Kantrowitz, not after his father Irving went to all that trouble to make people think they were born Unitarian? Sure, it sounds like a bleached blonde stripper or a Tri Delt from Ole Miss, but it's who I've been since I was 22 and by the time we split up it was the kids' last name, too. Besides, let's face it, people remember a name like that: "Sugar Kane? Oh yes, isn't she the one who did *Going It Alone*?" In L.A. people know you by your credits but a catchy handle don't hurt, as they say. (As *who* says, I can hear you asking, and as a matter of fact, it was a guy I once played gin rummy with all night when a snowstorm grounded every flight out of JFK).

Where's the woman who came in here a few hours ago with seventy nine pairs of shoes in her closet, one Emmy in a bathroom on West 79th Street and the other in a box in a basement in Laurel Canyon? Who's the broad with a picture of a blurry little shadow on an ultrasound in a corner of her bathroom mirror, who any second now is going to burst into tears because she just realized maybe she's never going to find out whether it's a boy or a girl, not to mention buying it that cute little leather jacket in the window of Baby Gap? What happened to her, huh? Or, as a great communicator and second-rate actor once said, "Where's the rest of Me?"

I didn't say any of that to Nurse Nancy, though—I'm not kidding, that was her name, it said so right on the tag over her pocket. I just said, I really have to pee, so could you please bring me a bedpan or disconnect me?

She unclipped the clothespin and steadied me while I stood up. I was a little weak in the knees but I made it to the bathroom. I splashed some cold water on my face and looked in the mirror over the sink, expecting a reasonable facsimile of my usual self—almond-shaped brown eyes and high cheekbones, the only valuables my great grandmother managed to take with her when she was chased out of Minsk in a pogrom; a mouth usually described as big even when it's closed, which isn't often, but which on anyone but a New Yorker would simply be called generous; light brown hair, only three days earlier streaked and highlighted with three different colors and layered and feathered into this year's version of the same medium short style I've worn most of my life except during my Carly Simon period.

But the woman who stared back at me in the unforgiving light of the bathroom didn't look like me. Her flesh seemed to have gone slack overnight and come loose from its moorings, especially under her eyes, which receded back into the sockets. The cartography of her face was different, too, as if a mighty river had overrun its banks and carved new channels into the surrounding landscape. Her skin was dry and crackled like parchment. She looked frail. She looked old.

Nurse Nancy helped me back into bed and smoothed the damp hair back from my forehead with a cool hand that smelled like the Jurgens lotion my *bubbe* Tessie used. When she was my age, she was already dead. Then I did cry—just a little.

"It's okay, you're going to be fine, really you are," said the nurse. Then she adjusted my blanket with a brisk snap and went out.

O'Neill hadn't changed his green pajamas. He looked like he'd been up all night, not saving lives but cramming for a final. I had shoes that were older than he was.

"When can I get out of here?"

"What's your hurry?" he said, like a policeman who's just pulled you over for speeding and really seems to hope you have a reason he hasn't heard before.

Since I didn't have one—I'm due at the White House, Aliens are chasing me, or even the only one that ever worked with a cop, I've just started my period and I have to get to a drug store—I asked if I could at least use the phone.

"Sorry, there are no phones in the CCU. The nurse will be glad to call for you if there's someone you need to reach."

"Thanks, but I'd just as soon do it myself. You didn't answer my question. When can I get out of here?"

"We'll move you out of here as soon as there's an aide to do it. We need the bed. But I want to make sure you're okay before I release you. Monitor things for a day or so, run a couple of tests. Who is your regular doctor?"

"Uh...I don't actually have one. Unless a plastic surgeon counts. I'm a very healthy person. Really."

"Is there someone at home to take care of you?"

"Why? Will I need to be taken care of?" Maybe Rosa, my once a week cleaning lady, could come in for a couple of days.

"It might not be a bad idea."

It would be a terrible one. "Why? How sick am I?"

"Your ECG looks pretty normal and there doesn't seem to be any major damage to the heart muscle. It may be just unstable angina. Were you exercising when you started to feel pain in your chest?"

I shook my head. "I don't do anything I can't do in three inch heels. What's unstable angina?"

"A temporary condition that happens when some of the heart muscle isn't getting enough blood. With a heart attack, the blood flow is cut off. If it were regular angina, you'd have a pattern of attacks, although not usually this severe. Have you felt anything like this before?"

"Never. Believe me, I'd have remembered. So it wasn't a heart attack? I'm okay?"

"I didn't say that. Stable or not, angina increases your risk of having a heart attack. Obviously you have some kind of cardiovascular disease.

That's not uncommon in women your age. Is there a history of heart disease in your family?"

I shook my head.

"Have you been under a lot of stress lately?"

"No more than usual."

"Do you smoke?"

"Not really."

He looked skeptical. "One or two a day," I admitted.

"Eat lot of fatty foods? Besides the kung pao chicken, that is."

"Hardly ever." Not if you didn't count pizza, pasta alfredo, and Krispy Cremes. "You know, the French, who eat a lot of fat, have fewer heart attacks than the British or Americans," I told him.

"You don't say. Do you drink?"

"Just red wine occasionally, with dinner. Italians, who drink excessive amounts of red wine, also suffer fewer heart attacks than the British or Americans."

"Your point being?"

"You might as well eat and drink what you like. It's speaking English that kills you."

"I'll keep that in mind." he said dryly. But he nearly smiled, which made me feel a little better. "So you don't get much exercise, huh?"

"You mean besides running off at the mouth and leaping to conclusions?" That got another smile—a real one this time. "Well, I walk my dog every day."

He made a few notes on a clipboard. "You need to get on a regular exercise program. Eat healthier. Stop smoking—entirely. And we'll put you on some medication. If you take sensible precautions, there's no reason you can't get this under control. We'll talk some more after we've run a few tests."

"I'm a little tired now. I think I'd like to sleep." I had a lot to think about. And if I went to sleep, I wouldn't have to.

O'Neill came in again after they moved me into a room at the opposite end of the floor from the CCU. I 'd had a chest x-ray and a stress test, blood drawn so many times by so many different people that I felt like a fugitive from an Anne Rice novel, and I was bored, hungry and cranky.

"You said I didn't have a heart attack, and you've taken enough blood for a vampire, can I go home now?"

"What? And miss dinner?" he replied, noting my untouched tray, which contained the kind of lunch you make for yourself the day after you try on bathing suits. "I want to get some pictures of your heart."

"Oh, drat, I left my 5 by 7's at home."

"Hmm. Yes. Well, I'm sure they would have been helpful."

He seemed to be waiting for me to ask him more questions, but I didn't. I wasn't uninterested—I just didn't want to know, not right then, anyway. Sooner or later I would have to, but since there wasn't anything I could do, any decisions to make, at least not yet, why bother?

"Well then, I'll see you in the cath lab later," he said. He took my cell phone from my hand and put it in the drawer of the night table. "Meanwhile, please use the hospital phone if you want to call someone."

Sure, and let everyone with caller ID know where I am. As soon as he left I retrieved my cell and scrolled down the numbers, then punched in Robin's. "There you are," she said, a reproof in her voice. If I hadn't reported in by the end of the day, she'd have sent out the Marines. "I've been trying to reach you. Hedley called. She said Nelly loved the script."

"She said that last week."

"Well, she said it again. It's still too early to get a commitment for the pilot, but she said everyone there is very high on it."

It would be two weeks before the networks announced. I hadn't made it to this stage with a series in fifteen years. If the pilot got made—if the talent was right—if the stars were aligned with the planets and the zeitgeist was with me and the network meant it when they said they were looking for a show exactly like this one, then maybe there was a chance.

"I've been thinking we should tweak it a little," Robin said. "That scene where Amelia has dinner with Jean Paul, before he realizes who she is, that could use some work."

"No tweaking. We gave it our best shot. Listen, Robin, I'm going out of town for a few days."

"What? Where are you going?"

"I haven't seen my mother in a couple of months, I thought I'd run down to Boca. I'll be back Sunday night."

"But what if we hear something? How will I reach you?"

"I'll be checking my messages. We won't hear anything. Don't worry."

Just then the hospital intercom went off. "Dr. Friedman to the ER, Dr. Friedman."

"What's that?" said Robin. "Where are you?"

"At the airport. Gotta' go, they're calling my flight."

I spent what seemed like the rest of the day on a wheeled table in a drafty hallway. No phone, no book or newspaper, not even *Oprah* and *Dr. Phil* to while the hours away. Finally a young Hispanic man in a green scrub suit that managed to cling to a beautiful pair of buns hooked me up to an IV pole. "What's that?" I asked, as he filled the flaccid plastic bag above my head.

"It's a sedative," he said. "A little Valium."

"A lot would be better," I replied, and he grinned.

A few minutes later he wheeled me into a room and positioned the table under a large camera that was hooked up to a flat screen computer monitor while a nurse pulled back the sheet covering my body from the waist down. She shaved a little hair from my groin, not that there was much of it left: My once thick, springy black bush looked like a stubby winter garden these days. I'd heard Melatonin was good for that; I don't usually need anything to help me sleep but I'd been meaning to pick up a bottle of the pills at Duane Reed and see if I could coax my pussy hair back. Then she sprayed something cold where she'd shaved me.

"This will only sting for a second," said O'Neill, sticking a needle down there. Behind the surgical mask his eyes looked sympathetic, which I didn't take as a good thing; I liked it better when he was being a smart ass, or even a stuffed shirt.

"I don't usually get this personal on a first date," I told him.

"Neither does he," muttered a nurse standing next to him. The technician chuckled, and O'Neill blushed all the way to his receding hairline. It was a regular little *Gray's Anatomy* in there.

Four small monitors were strategically positioned around the table. "We're taking pictures of your arteries. In a few minutes, you can see them," O'Neil explained.

"Don't bother," I said. "I never take a good picture. The camera hates me." I closed my eyes, gave myself up to the Valium, floated off to fantasyland, and barely noticed when they rolled me back to my room.

By the time O'Neill came in, though, I was wide awake, hung over and really starving this time. Visions of soup dumplings from Joe's Shanghai danced in my head and I was seriously considering ordering them in. All Nurse Nancy'd brought me was a pitcher of water, which she refilled twice. "You want to clear the dye from the rest out of your system," she told me, and consequently I'd been peeing almost constantly since being wheeled back to my room.

O'Neill was Mr. Efficiency this time—no small talk, he'd probably used up his quota with me already. "You had minor blockage in one chamber," he said.

"The House or the Senate?"

He ignored what I personally thought was a snappy comeback. "One of your arteries was about 20 percent closed. That's what's causing the angina. You didn't have an infarct. There's no damage to the heart muscle...not yet. You were very lucky."

Great. I should have bought that lottery ticket yesterday.

"You can go home tonight if you want to, although I'd advise you to wait until tomorrow," he said.

"Oh, damn, I'm supposed to go hang gliding tomorrow."

"There's no wind forecast, you might as well cancel it and go mountain climbing instead." Well, maybe he did have a sense of humor in there somewhere. A person can be smart, interesting, accomplished and attractive, but if they can't laugh, especially at themselves, they'll never get very far with me. "I want you to take it easy for a few days," he added. "Only short walks at first. Don't exert yourself. Eat regularly, take your medication, and try to avoid stress."

"What about sex?" I asked.

I don't know why I said that—to make sure he noticed I wasn't ready for the senior scrap pile yet? To reassure myself? I could tell he was embarrassed—women probably didn't ask him that question very often, or maybe the idea of someone who was old enough to be his mother having sex unnerved him.

"Maybe not for a few days, but after that there's no reason you can't resume your, uh, normal schedule." When it came to sex, my normal schedule was seldom to rarely, something I tried not to obsess about.

"I'd like to get out of here tonight," I told him. "Is there any real reason I shouldn't?"

"I'll get the nurse to give you your discharge instructions," he said, "although I think you'd be better off getting a good night's sleep."

"My sentiments exactly," I said. "What kind of instructions?"

"Diet, exercise, medication, that kind of thing. Just use your common sense. I want to see you in my office in two weeks, unless you have more chest pain. If that happens, come in immediately. Don't ignore it. Heart disease kills more women than breast cancer. And you might ask whoever's taking you home to stick around till tomorrow."

"Is that necessary?"

"No, but it's not a bad idea. It'll keep you from worrying."

"I'm not worried." I stared at him defiantly.

"Good," he said. "Right now there's no need to be. Call my office in the morning and set up your follow up appointment."

It was close to eight o'clock when the aide wheeled me downstairs to the front door. A cab was just pulling up. Stuffing the discharge instructions and the pills from the hospital pharmacy into the pocket of my jacket, I got in. The interior smelled like cheap perfume and Mexican food, so I opened the window and breathed in fresh New York air—roasted nuts, exhaust fumes, dog pee, brine, and excitement. We were stuck behind another taxi, and I watched people hurrying past on the street, never making eye contact with each other, intent on their errands or plans, wondering if the video store had the DVD they wanted or how to tell the wife they'd just been fired or whether that guy they gave their number to in the bar last night would really call. Rap music blared from boom boxes and passing car radios, and horns blared in response and somewhere someone shouted, "Watch it, mother fucker."

I sucked it all in greedily. It felt like I'd come back after a long absence. *Back from the dead.* You're being an idiot, I told myself, and gave the driver my address.

CHAPTER
THREE

When I came in Mrs. B. was in the lobby, replacing someone's copy of *Time*—she does that, darts in and out of her apartment when she thinks nobody's looking and borrows other people's magazines from the table next to the mailboxes. She puts them back after she's read them, but by the time I get my *New York* the "Sales and Bargains" column is out of date.

Caught in the act, she went on the offensive. "You look terrible," she said.

"Thank you for that vote of confidence, Mrs. B," I said. "By the way, have you finished my *Vanity Fair* yet?"

"I don't know what you're talking about," she said, scuttling away like a pigeon, which in fact she resembled, with her pouter bosom and tiny feet in their clunky black shoes. *Nice going, Sugar, next you'll be taking candy from babies.*

Once inside my apartment I sank heavily into the couch. Tory jumped into my lap, sniffing my unfamiliar antiseptic smell and fretting at the plastic strip on my wrist. I felt her body shaking the way it does when something spooks her, and nuzzled my face next to hers. "It's okay, sweetie, it's okay," I said soothingly.

A dog is the perfect relationship for a single woman. It loves you unconditionally, even when you haven't brushed your teeth yet, it doesn't hog the remote or ask you for money, and it gets you off your ass and out of the house at least a couple of times a day. Unlike cats, who give their affection sparingly and on their own terms, dogs have no boundaries; they come when you call them, not when they feel like it, which makes them my kind of pet.

I never expected to own a dog again, but I woke up one morning with a powerful urge to complicate my life, which for a long time had been blessedly free of responsibility for anything more demanding than a philodendron. I didn't have the patience for a puppy—I was tempted, but I knew better. While they're cute for a few months, pretty soon everything you own has been chewed into confetti or dotted with yellow rings. "What I want is a grown dog," I told Peggy. "Healthy, housebroken, and trained. Like a well-behaved teenager that somebody else raised."

Peggy found Tory for me at a kennel near her country house in Woodstock. "She's a six year old spayed female," she said. "The owner's looking for a good home for her. She used to be their best breeder, but she's been replaced by a younger bitch."

"Haven't we all?"

Peggy has a Portuguese water dog named Jung, a sweet, slightly goofy animal I'm very fond of, so we went to the kennel where she got him to meet Tory. The first time I saw her she took my measure, sizing me up with startlingly blue eyes that gleamed with intelligence. Then she inclined her head slightly as if to say, We're beyond all that pet and master nonsense, aren't we? and bounded into my lap with a single graceful leap, her snaky black Medusa-like curls quivering under my touch just like they were doing right now.

That was five years ago. It's trite to say a dog is your soul mate, and if I heard anyone I knew make that statement I'd think, how sad—that's like thinking the people in your favorite TV series are your friends, which of course is what we *want* you to think. But Tory is incredibly tuned in to my emotional frequency, as if I'm broadcasting feelings only she can pick up. So maybe she was spooked by the sense that something about me was different, the same way I was—sort of.

We weren't the only ones. The readout on my answering machine indicated that Paul had called six times—the first time, I noted, was at 7:30 the previous night, just when the octopus was doing its thing. That must have been the call I couldn't answer.

There was a message from Jessie, too, but it didn't sound urgent, just whiny, and since I didn't think I could drudge up the requisite empathy, I put off returning it. Paul, though—that call wouldn't wait. While Jessie sometimes seems to read my mind, Paul knows me—knows us all—on a deeper, more visceral level. Since he was a kid he's always had an uncanny sense of our physical selves; he knew when one of us was sick or hurt almost before we knew it ourselves. Once I was in a car accident, and Paul told Ted about it even before I did, which was after I'd been X-rayed and had my wrist set. And there was the time Jessie was at summer camp in Nova Scotia, and Paul, hundreds of miles away, called us to say there was something wrong with her just before the camp director notified us that she'd been taken to the hospital with appendicitis.

"Hi, darling," I trilled gaily when he answered the phone. "Sorry I didn't call you back earlier—I've been in the country at Peggy's for a couple of days."

He sounded relieved. "That's good. I had this...you know, my thing."

"Really? I'm fine, honey. I'm really fine. Maybe you're tuned into somebody else's old lady."

"It sure felt like it was you. I talked to Jessie and she said the baby had been kicking the hell out of her, but otherwise she was okay."

"You didn't tell her you were worried about me, did you?"

" 'Course not," he said.

"Did you talk to your father, too?"

"Uh uh." Paul had never quite forgiven Ted for dumping me—his loyalty warmed me like a sweater on a chilly night.

"How are you? Anything new in your life? Or anyone?" I chose my words carefully, lest he think I was "pressuring" him. Peggy, who's a therapist, once said of a mutual friend whose son has never lived up to their expectations, "It must be hard to always be told how much potential you have. It must be easier just not to do anything, for fear you won't meet all those expectations." She wasn't talking about Paul—at least I don't think she was—but her words hit me with a powerful jolt of insight into my own child.

"Just pounding nails," he said. Paul dropped out of UC halfway through and never went back. Whenever the subject of how he's wasting his life comes up, my mother says, "What did you think would happen when you told him to do what he wanted as long as it made him happy? Whoever said you're supposed to be happy?" I don't get defensive any more, I just change the subject. Paul, who's 30, pretty much treats the future as if it's the present that just hasn't happened yet. But at least he's not in jail or on the streets, a couple of alternate lifestyles I pondered more than once as he made his leisurely way toward adulthood.

There were a few other messages but nothing that couldn't wait, so I filled the big old-fashioned claw-footed tub, which is one of the best things about my apartment besides the rent, and tossed in a couple of capfuls of *Badedas*. I lit a cigarette and took a long drag, immersing myself up to my neck in the hot foamy water. I always had my last cigarette of the day in the tub: My New Year's resolution this year had been to give up giving up smoking, and I was sticking to it. The visitation from the octopus was not going to change that, or anything else.

Later, in bed, I watched Letterman's monologue and then I snapped off the TV and picked up the book I'd been reading when the octopus struck. It was another of those novels whose time seems suddenly to have arrived, about a group of women taking the body or the ashes of their friend on its final journey. Hag lit, Suzanne calls it—the new publishing zeitgeist, all these stories of college roommates whose lives have gone in unexpected ways confronting the distance from their youth and their own mortality when the first of them dies.

My mother used to steer the conversation away from topics that were unpleasant or threatened to provoke a fight by saying, "The subject is not of general interest." That was exactly how I felt, so I dropped the book on the floor, turned off the light and turned over. Tory snuggled up closer next to me, and we called it a night.

....

"You said you'd be here when the baby was born."

"I know, and I will be. But that's still two months off. Have you seen the doctor this week? What did he say?"

"The usual. Everything's fine, don't worry, take your vitamins, go out with your husband for dinner and a movie while you still can. *As if!*"

My grown-up daughter sounded more like a grumpy teenager than a woman in the last trimester of pregnancy. My son-in-law Zach is a talented chef who plans to open his own restaurant one of these days, which means dining out is research, not romance. He already has two willing investors ready to back him—the befoodifuls, Jessie calls them, some wealthy Angelenos who've followed Zach's career from the little bistro in the Valley where he was a sous-chef when Jessie met him to a bigger job at a restored Hollywood landmark and finally to his present position as executive chef at a restaurant so exclusive it has an unlisted phone number and no prices on the menu. But when it's your own restaurant, you don't leave at seven or take two consecutive days off, so 'one of these days' is somewhere in the future, between the baby's arrival and his high school graduation. Jessie's been on maternity leave for most of her pregnancy—she's an artist's rep for a big music label, which means late nights at smoky clubs. It's not the best atmosphere for a mother-to-be, especially one who's already had two miscarriages, and although she vows to return after the baby is born, once she has a real baby to care for she may be less interested in the tantrums and demands of the overgrown ones she works with.

She sounded lonely and exasperated and bored, but I resisted the impulse to say, Well why don't I come out and keep you company? I was tempted; it wouldn't hurt to be in L.A. when the network made the decision about the pilot, and I really didn't have anything else planned. But then I remembered the two steep flights of stairs you have to climb just to get to the front door of Zach and Jessie's rented house in Echo Park, and the three other flights once you're inside. I am an old hand at wrestling mother guilt to the ground—unlike other kinds, it leaves stretch marks and never goes away—so I told her I'd see her soon and rang off.

By late that afternoon, a cold front had blown in, reason enough to spend the weekend inside, on the couch or in bed, dozing and reading and watching old movies on TV. I didn't feel much like talking to anyone, so I let the messages pile up on the answering machine and turned off my cell phone. Later, when I figured the callers wouldn't be home, I'd ring back, say "Phone tag—you're it, catch you later," and hang up.

Writers aren't solitary by nature, at least I'm not, but sometimes you just have to hang around yourself in order to do the work. If I'm on deadline I do the phone tag thing, but otherwise I reach out and touch someone a few times a day, just to get out of my own head. That weekend I didn't talk to anyone, but every time I heard the phone ring I felt a small twinge of reassurance. I'd never be one of those paragraphs in the *Daily News*, someone whose dead body isn't discovered until the smell alerts the neighbors. Not that I haven't played that scenario in my mind before—I don't know any single woman who hasn't. But this time it seemed to resonate on a different frequency.

By Monday I was feeling a lot more like myself, so I spent the morning putting the final touches on a rewrite for a *Lifetime* movie based on a best-selling novel about a murdered teenager who manages to send her clever younger sister clues from the great beyond about the identity of her killer. Then I surfed the Web for a few minutes. Google had millions of hits about heart disease, but after I clicked on a couple, I realized I really didn't want to know any more than I already did, which is definitely not like me. I am an information junkie, a research hound since my first job as a fact checker at the *New Yorker*; if you needed an answer on the Sunday Double Crostic or a Life Line on *Who Wants to Be a Millionaire*, I'm the one you'd call, and if I didn't already know the answer I'd mouse it up in a nanosecond.

I closed out of Windows, fixed a tuna sandwich and tackled my bills.

You know you've become a woman of a certain age when the anxiety dream about oversleeping your SAT's turns into the one about being a middle class bag lady. Until I sold the article to the *L.A. Weekly*, which led to the book, which sank like a stone until it came to the attention of a TV agent, who put me together with a producer...well, at least that far back, when I was regretting not giving into the impulse to bankrupt the Tortmaster for his misdeeds, I was skilled and devious in the art of stretching a free-lancer's occasional paydays well past the second or third notice from a creditor. I'd "forget" to sign my name on an otherwise clearly written check or I'd purposely put the pediatrician's payment in the envelope addressed to the dentist. When someone called from Delinquent Accounts, I'd identify myself as the baby-sitter, all the while wondering what those accounts did when no one was looking—joyride in borrowed cars, knock up teenage girls, get kicked out of high school?

The show changed all that, and I'd had a good run in the stock market, but those days were gone and money was getting to be a headache again. I wrote out checks for the taxes on the L.A. house that were due at the end of the month, which was also when my tenant's lease expired, and for my health insurance, whose first bill of the new year came with a particularly unpleasant addendum this time- not just the usual rate raise but a notice that this year my very own personal hike included a "decade surcharge."

I had had a very good time in my financial go-go days, indulging myself and those I loved in ways large and small. But as I wrote out the checks I wondered, not for the first time, what I'd do if the network didn't green light the new show, which was far from a sure thing. The only other possibilities I could conjure up that might save me from my reckless financial ways—winning the lottery or finding a rich husband—were equally improbable...given the odds on getting a pilot made, let alone a series, I'd have a better shot at either of those.

The house in Laurel Canyon, which I got in the divorce and where I raised the kids, was supposed to be my hedge against growing old in poverty. But I'd refinanced so often there probably wasn't enough equity left in it to keep me for more than a few years—another stupid decision in the low interest, high flying days of the tech boom, when I borrowed on margin to finance my indulgences. When it all came to a crashing halt, I took a big hit in the pocketbook, but unfortunately, my spending habits didn't change, too. I just went on merrily living on the come—the next big deal was coming soon, and after that one failed to materialize or went south, well, there would always be another one...that's the Hollywood line, equal parts hope and hype, and it's an easy one to fall for when you're young.

In fact, The *Lifetime* script was the only deal my agent had made for me in so long I'd started to worry that he'd drop me as a client. Sandro's hints about how TV is a young person's game these days weren't entirely lost on me—how could they be, given his hair plugs, Botox, and the personal trainer he'd put on his payroll? According to him it wasn't just the talent that was getting younger and younger—"It's the creatives, too," he said, "the writers, directors and producers. That kid who's running New Line now? I haven't finished paying for his *bar mitzvah* present yet."

Sandro's last big deal for me was Lexy's autobiography. He made sure I got my advance up front, which was smart since *Love, Lexy*—her title, not mine—was on the remainder table a few months after it was published. Lexy went from starring in *Going It Alone* for six seasons to a couple of other series that never made it beyond thirteen weeks. In between there were a couple of stints in rehab and almost as many relapses, romances, come-backs and fade-outs as Liza's, which made a tell-all attractive to enough publishers to bid the proposal up to six figures at an auction. Not that the book wasn't a carefully varnished version of "all"—if I'd put in everything I knew about Lexy, she'd be lucky to get signed for a supermarket opening.

But that money was going fast, too. By now my net worth was anorexic enough to make the *Times'* "Neediest Cases" nightmare a recurring feature of my REM sleep, like every woman who's not independently wealthy or even dependently, which is more often the case. It was also a depressing thought in the middle of an otherwise sunny day, so I dealt with it the way I usually do—I headed for Filene's Basement.

It was a little longer than I'd walked since coming home from the hospital, but I was feeling okay, even pretty good, until I made my way to the register with a pair of last season Blahniks. I didn't need blue satin shoes—who does?—but they were so cheap it would have been a crime not to buy them. That's when I bumped into Carrie.

"Sugar, when did you get back, what's going on? Robin said you were in Boca, I finally called her, and I've been leaving messages since Thursday! We had lunch Wednesday and you never said you were going away—did something happen to Frances?"

Carrie is one of my best friends. She's a professor of medieval literature at Columbia, although her deep, husky voice could earn her a fortune doing phone sex, which she swears she's going to take up when academic politics finally drive her out of her sixth floor office in Philosophy Hall. The English department at Columbia is notoriously awful for women, so much so that even a distinguished scholar like Carolyn Heilbrun finally gave up and went back to writing mysteries about a college professor instead of being one.

Carrie is married to a writer who has great hopes for posthumous recognition, since he believes the world is not ready for his genius yet. In a good month Geoffrey ekes out six pages, and then spends the next one and the one after that rewriting them, so he doesn't publish more than once a decade, and Carrie supports them. Despite his intellectual pretensions, I love Geoffrey—he's a bear of a man with a booming laugh and hearty good nature that belies the dark, tightly constricted novels he writes. A superb cook and a great raconteur who knows his way around the cleaning products aisle of Duane Reade, he has the sexual staying power of a man half his age. At least that's what Carrie says. They're an odd-looking couple; he's enormous, and she's barely five feet tall, thin and wiry with no excess flesh on her bones. Her hair is more silver than black now, shorter than she used to wear it; it curls around her face and softens her square, slightly pugnacious jaw, so that when she contradicts Geoffrey or teases him about his self-importance, she reminds me of a Scottie nipping at a grizzly.

Of all the people I wasn't ready to face yet, at least not till I had the tale of the octopus ready for public consumption, Carrie was first on my list. We talk to each other every day, and usually have coffee a couple of times a week at the Starbucks between my apartment and hers. There's hardly anything we don't tell each other—the good, the bad, and the dish—and if I'd called anyone from the emergency room, it would have been her. "We didn't think you'd miss the party unless it was an emergency. Is she okay?"

Oh, shit...that's what all those calls over the weekend were about. I'd completely spaced Suzanne's sixtieth birthday extravaganza.

Carrie and I had been planning it for months. We'd already celebrated Suzanne's actual birthday the week before at a hugely indulgent lunch at Café des Artistes, where we finished every crumb on the dessert sampler and then ordered another, because Suzanne, the first of us to hit the big six oh said that age had its privileges, among them the right to indulge ourselves in everything bad for us that we gave up years ago, like smoking, drinking, recreational drugs and chocolate mousse.

` "When Jackie Onassis found out she had cancer, she said what she regretted most were those hundred sit-ups she used to do every day," she told us. "She told Nan Talese if she'd known that was what was going to happen she wouldn't have bothered." Suzanne is an editor at Doubleday. We met when I was ghosting Lexy's book and I introduced her to Carrie.

I couldn't believe I'd forgotten the party, especially since I'd made the arrangements to have it in that penthouse with the pool where Samantha was romanced by her rich boss on *Sex and the City*. I'd called in a favor from a location manager I knew, who got it for us practically free—which is to say, as much as I'd spend on Suzanne's birthdays and Christmases if we both lived to be a hundred.

I hoped the octopus hadn't affected my brain as well as my heart, because I had one New York minute, which goes by quicker here than it does anywhere else, to come up with an emergency that would satisfy Carrie, not to mention Suzanne.

"Frances had a stroke." I hoped God wasn't listening, even though I don't believe in Him and know that even if I did, thinking doesn't mean happening. And it wasn't an unconscious wish on my part, either...even if my mother can be a pain in the ass sometimes, I'm not ready for her to die yet. Peggy, who used to be a Freudian analyst, says it's difficult to mourn an ambivalently held object, so I should settle my unfinished business with Frances while I still can, which is easy for Peggy to say because she's not her mother. "Don't worry, she's fine now," I added, more to reassure myself than allay Carrie's concerns. "She just thought she had a stroke. Or Esme did, anyway." Esme is my mother's maid, confidante and companion—she moved from New Jersey to Florida with Frances after my father died, and she's practically one of the family. "Turns out she'd played nine holes of golf that morning in 90 degree weather, and she hadn't eaten all day—you know Frances, she's was a bulimic before they knew what it was, she still takes ExLax every night."

"She does?" Carrie wrinkled her nose in distaste.

"Mm, she says it's because she doesn't have time to wait for her bowels to move. Anyway, she fainted, and Esme got scared because when she came to she didn't remember what happened. Esme called me right after she called 911, so I ran down there...I didn't even take my cell phone."

"Is she still in the hospital?"

"By the time I got there she was abusing the nurses and demanding a cigarette and a glass of scotch. They kept her overnight for observation, and then we got her home and settled in, but I couldn't get a flight back until late last night. God, I'm sorry. You think Suzanne will ever forgive me?"

"We were both pretty worried, especially when you did that, 'You're it' thing with the phones. You only do that when you really don't want to talk."

It always surprises me when my little tricks don't fool the people who know me best. "I'll call her as soon as I get home. I'll send flowers. I'll clean her closets. I'll get her kid's movie into Sundance," I said.

"Sure you will. You really ought to talk to a therapist about your grandiosity," Carrie said dryly. "You buying those?" she asked, eyeing the Blahniks. "What, there's an old bridesmaid's dress in your closet you've been saving for a special occasion, only you didn't have the shoes to go with it?"

"Hope springs eternal," I replied. "You want to go get a latte?"

CHAPTER
FOUR

I usually call Frances on Sunday mornings—we do the *Times* crossword puzzle together on the phone, which means I feed her the answers and she says, "I knew that, it just slipped my mind for a minute."

"You didn't call yesterday," she said reprovingly.

"I'm really sorry...I got involved in stuff and by the time I remembered, it was too late to call you. I haven't even looked at the puzzle yet."

"It was an easy one this week—I got most of it done before my coffee was cold," she said. "I thought maybe you met some nice man at Suzanne's party and went home with him." The mythical Prince Charming—someone Frances still hopes will appear and save me from my ignominious single state—is the only acceptable excuse for not calling my mother on Sunday mornings. "I hope you didn't sleep with him—not on the first date, even at your age. *Especially* at your age," she added.

"As *if*," I said—why do I always sound like my own kid when I'm talking to her? Peggy says it's a form of infantile regression, and that's probably true, because the closer I get to Frances, the younger I become. When I see her, and even sometimes when we just talk, I feel like that fat, uncoordinated nine year old who couldn't do anything right except get good grades in school and make her laugh. Which wasn't enough for my mother—beauty and popularity were what counted with her, at least for her daughters. Her son, whom she thought destined for success, prestige and wealth, disappointed her, too.

My brother is a high school teacher who lives in Oregon with his born-again wife; they raise llamas and seem perfectly content with their lives, which Frances considers evidence that Pete is as crazy as my sister Joan, who spent her young adulthood dropping in and out of psychiatric hospitals until she was appropriately medicated with lithium. Neither one has lived up to my mother's expectations that her children reflect well on her. By default, I'm the only one who even approaches that—at least I've written a few books, been on *Oprah* and *Phil Donahue*, and had a hit TV show for a few years, which almost makes up for divorcing Ted without getting a good settlement.

My mother is one of those people who uses up all the oxygen in the room. It's not that the conversation is always all about her, but she experiences any of her children's shortcomings as narcissistic insults—to her, not us—and she tends to dwell on them: my barren romantic life; my son's failure to graduate from college; my sister's weight problem, which is much more important in Frances's scheme of things that her mental instability; Pete's career choices; and his wife's disinterest in clothes and makeup, let alone her religious views. Conversely, our accomplishments belong to Frances, not us; like Joan finishing her Ph.D. at age 40 and going on to a successful career as an educational consultant; Pete growing his llama herd into a nice little sideline; his home-schooled son graduating from MIT at nineteen; Jessie snagging an ambitious, handsome husband; or me getting an Emmy.

"So how was the party?" Frances wanted to know. "What did you wear? It was so sweet of Suzanne to invite me—I sent her flowers, you know. Did she like them?"

"She loved them—that was very thoughtful of you, Mom."

"You know how fond of her I am...she was so kind when Daddy died. So how was it?"

I regaled her with the details Carrie had given me about the party and a few more I confabulated, and when we hung up, I was clenching my jaw the way Jessie does when she's shining me on to keep me from finding out stuff I'm better off not knowing.

By the middle of the week I'd almost forgotten about the false alarm, which was my take on the episode with the octopus. In spite of coming awake a few times in the middle of the night and taking my pulse or thinking twice before I had a cigarette (and then having it anyway), I was well into denial. I think denial, along with its first cousin, repression, is unfairly maligned; it's actually a pretty effective way of dealing with shit when it happens. But clearly Dr. O'Neill, whose receptionist called to schedule me for a follow-up, didn't think it was as useful a method of coping with life as I do.

His office was in a medical building two blocks from the hospital. The magazines in his waiting room didn't tell me much about him—the usual newsweeklies, *National Geographic*, *Men's Health*, and *Sail*. The art on the walls ran to well-framed photographs of six meter racing yachts and Ansel Adams studies of Yosemite. There were a half dozen other people already there; I gave my name to the receptionist, who weighed me and took my blood pressure, then handed me a form on a clipboard and motioned me to a seat.

It was a kind of medical history—actually, it said "Lifestyle Factors and Heart Disease", a nice cheery headline if I ever read one. I checked all the boxes that applied—well, mostly all. I was a little more honest about the cigarettes than I was in the hospital—*face it, Sugar, you smoke a pack a day, who are you kidding?* The alcohol questions weren't a problem—I'd rather spend my discretionary calories on cheesecake than booze, and if I'm somewhere I have to order a drink, I nurse along a single cassis or a glass of wine at dinner.

"Do you or have you used any of the following substances in the last year?" gave me pause. Was my occasional toke of pot a risk factor for heart disease, and was it any of O'Neill's business? You can't really keep anything private these days, especially not medical records, so I checked "not applicable" with one big mark that took in the whole depressing category.

I put "occasionally" on the question about sex, and upped my number of recent sexual partners to "one", which was only true in my dreams, unless "recent" meant two years ago. I left "current medications" mostly blank—I still had the pills I'd gotten from the hospital pharmacy, but I wasn't sure what they were or where I'd put them.

The exercise part didn't take long. I really ought to do something about that, like drag the Nordik Trak out of the other bedroom where it's covered by a pile of clothes and put it in front of the TV where I won't be able to ignore it.

I scrutinized the food section—maybe on the way home, I'd stop at Whole Foods, it was right on the way. Plenty of salad greens and fresh fruit, maybe some fish—I was already feeling so virtuous that when the nurse took the clipboard and beckoned me into O'Neill's office a few minutes later I wasn't prepared for the disapproving look on his face.

"I don't think you realize that this is a serious situation," he said. "Your blood pressure is higher than it should be, you should weigh fifteen pounds less, and your cholesterol is very problematic—you're not taking the medication, are you? And you're still smoking, I see. If you continue this way, the next cardiac event could kill you."

I was formulating a good retort—"We all have to go sometime," maybe?—when to my complete dismay and utter embarrassment, I burst into tears; unlike most men, it didn't faze O'Neill at all, and also unlike a shrink's office, his didn't have one lousy box of Kleenex.

He looked bored while I sniffled a few times and downright disapproving when I wiped my nose on the back of my sleeve.

"What will it take to convince you to start paying attention to your health?" he asked. "Do you not know that heart disease is the leading killer of women, especially women your age?"

Actually, I didn't—was there a ribbon for heart disease like there was for AIDS and breast cancer? Did I have one? Did I want one? I tried to compose myself by looking at the diplomas on the wall. He'd graduated from medical school later than I'd thought and I calculated that he probably wasn't more than a few years younger than the last man I had sex with. Not that O'Neill was my type. *But neither was that other guy—what if he turns out to be the last one I ever—*

"Is there something wrong?" he asked, interrupting my depressing conjecture. "You look uncomfortable."

"Sorry, just...you were saying?"

"I see here you're a writer and producer. For who?"

I resisted the urge to correct his grammar. "I'm in television."

"A pretty stressful job, I suppose."

"More when I'm not doing it than when I am. I have a show in the works...it's the waiting around for it to start that's stressful, not the work itself." Which wasn't exactly true; I was writing the show as well as running it, which wouldn't be any day at the beach, and if the series based on the pilot resulted, I'd be co-producing it as well.

"And you have a family...two children, is that right?"

"And a grandchild on the way," I added—I'd already crossed him off my "maybe" list anyway.

He brightened. "Well, that ought to give you a reason to take better care of yourself."

To be charitable, he probably thought that was encouraging, but it only made me sadder. Of course I was looking forward to the baby, but was that enough to live for? What about all those other things I'd never gotten around to doing? Maybe I was too old to be the First Woman Who, or learn to speak fluent French, climb Mt. Everest, write a great novel or even a good one, but if I really wanted to do any of those things, wouldn't I have done them already? Come to think of it, my life list was pretty outdated these days; I was no longer interested in backpacking around Europe or being

Mick Jagger's squeeze. And the big item that was still numero uno—finding the love of my life—didn't look like it might ever happen.

I suppose I thought Ted was that person when he took the ring out of the Cartier box and placed it on my finger; it was so long ago I can't remember. Or maybe it was simply time to get on with being a grown-up; everyone else I knew was married, and I'd always planned to have my children before I was 30. Ted Kane was smart, funny, out of Harvard undergrad and Columbia Law, and he almost looked Unitarian, with his blonde hair and straight nose. In addition to those attributes, he was crazy about me.

But not forever, as it turned out. The first few times he cheated I overlooked it and went on massive self-improvement campaigns—if it was my fault, which it must be, I could fix it. It wasn't, or so my shrink told me, but since the divorce, none of my relationships had worked out much better than my marriage. What I'd mostly learned in the analysis that was my fortieth birthday present to myself was that I'd never been loved the way I deserved to be loved—wholly, completely and unconditionally. Not by Frances, my father, or any of my boyfriends, both before and after Ted.

Until what Peggy calls my naturally oppositional personality asserted itself I was very good at being whoever a man wanted me to be. Since Ted fooled me by pretending to be a *mensch*, I've been more attracted to the ones who don't and aren't. "I like men with edges," I once told my shrink, "you know, difficult ones with complex personalities."

"Mmm," she said, "the kind who tend to criticize, control, or both."

"Well...sort of."

"Edges are just something you cut yourself on," she said. "Is that really what you want?"

Well, yes and no, I told her. "What I really want is for someone to love me the right way."

I still wanted that, and everything O'Neill said made me realize once again that if it hadn't happened yet, it probably wasn't ever going to.

It wasn't that I didn't want to be a grandmother—I just knew that that wasn't going to be enough. I didn't say that to O'Neill, though. "I'd like to see you in three months, unless you have any symptoms before then," he said. "I expect to see some positive change by that time. After all, relatively speaking, you've still got plenty of good years left."

CHAPTER
FIVE

My cell phone rang as I was leaving O'Neill's office. It was Zach, calling from another doctor's office three thousand miles away.

"She started spotting and having contractions, but it was a false alarm," said my son-in-law. "Dr. Levine wants her on full bed rest from now on, but she says she'll go nuts if she has to stay in the hospital for the next two months. My mother can probably help out, but—"

Stacy Stillerman's idea of helping out would be regaling Jessie with dire warnings about every potential obstetrical or pediatric disaster and sending her maid over to clean Jessie's house. Not that it couldn't use it—things fall off her and Zach like a deciduous tree, you can follow their trail from the front door to the bedroom, and while the kitchen in Zach's restaurant is as clean as an operating room, I wouldn't be surprised if the board of health closed down the one in his house.

Jessie can't stand Stacy, which secretly pleases me—no competition there—and even Zach can only tolerate his mother in small doses.

"Do you want me to come?"

"Oh, God, would you?" The relief in his voice was as thick as his béarnaise sauce. Was there any choice? Of course not. By the next morning I was winging my way west, having hastily thrown some clothes in a suitcase, packed up my laptop, and cancelled out of a panel at the 92nd Street Y with the cliterati—Nora, Erica, Vanessa and me, one dame each from movies, books, theater and television, plus Candice Bergen. I don't get that many chances to pontificate publicly about why there are no uppity women characters on TV anymore, especially not in such exalted company; I'd probably been a fill-in for Linda Bloodworth Thomas or Diane English, but it was a chance to remind the power dames that I was still around, and also to schmooze Candice. I wanted her to play Amelia, the elegant, charming and still sexy widow who rules her very private inquiry firm—and her headstrong twenty-something daughter, a computer whiz with a pierced nose, a sloppy wardrobe and a smart mouth—with the proverbial velvet-gloved iron hand. Until she turned a guest arc into a steady role on *Boston Legal*, she hasn't had her own series since *Murphy Brown*, and even she, Spader and Shatner together won't be able to keep that one alive much longer. Also, the script of my pilot happens to feature the theft of an illegally acquired Old Master from a chateau in France, where she used to live. That wasn't a coincidence— I'd had Candice in mind for Amelia from the beginning. I'd planned to casually slip her the script after the panel, since if she were interested it would go a long way toward convincing the pilot gods to smile on me.

Before I left for the west coast I e-mailed my tenants and asked them to charge up the battery on my old BMW. I've hung onto it since I bought it after *Going It Alone* went into syndication; I keep it in the garage in Laurel Canyon, thus avoiding the temptation to rent the latest statusmobile when I land in L.A.

I unloaded Tory from her travel kennel at the airport and we took a cab home. When I moved back to New York ten years ago, I moved some of my things into the studio at the back of the property, renting the house itself to a couple of newly minted lawyers who've acquired twins, partnerships, and their own mortgage in the interim. Whether I re-rent it or not, sooner rather than later I'll have to tackle the big-ticket maintenance I've been postponing—a new roof, a new paint job, and probably a new drain field, too, given the temper tantrums mother nature so often unleashes on southern California. But until I've got the money and time to deal with it, my little studio will do fine.

Nobody was home, but the front yard was littered with packing boxes, and there was a note on the windshield of the freshly washed car welcoming me back—another reminder that I was in California now, since nobody in New York ever does anything that nice for their landlord. It almost makes up for the deflation of self esteem, like a slow leak in an old tire, that afflicts me when I first get back here and everything I'm wearing seems hopelessly out of date, every one of my excess pounds is glaringly evident, and everyone I see is at least two generations younger than I am.

I put my suitcase in the trunk of the Beemer next to my dusty gym bag, which was stuffed with workout clothes so old they probably hadn't even invented spandex when I acquired them. I'd succumbed to one of those occasional impulses that affects every woman after she's been dumped by a man and purchased a lifetime membership in a health club in Westwood Village, which I resolved I'd reacquaint myself with unless it had been replaced by a trendy new restaurant featuring pan-Balkan fusion cuisine. I'd need some new gym clothes, too. But you can't buy those unless you can wear them without looking like you need them, which sounds as ridiculous as cleaning the house before the maid comes, but makes perfect sense in southern California.

I unlocked the door of the studio and filled a water bowl for Tory, then let her sniff around the not unfamiliar yard, stopping here and there to pee in exactly the same places she always did, even though it was more than a year since she'd come to California with me. I breathed in the familiar sun-warmed scents of orange and jasmine, the slight metallic undertone that's like a little reminder that California isn't really paradise, even though it seems that way when you've just arrived from somewhere else, especially New York. As I stood there, not really thinking about anything, feeling the soft air settle around me and fitting myself back into the place where I'd carelessly spent so many years I'd never get back, time reeled backward, flashing momentarily like a strobe lighting up a dark room. ... A fourth of July barbecue the summer we bought the house, the night I went into labor with Paul and suddenly realized my life was about to change and there was nothing I could do about it, the day John Lennon was shot and Ted told me he was leaving while I sat in front of the TV watching the crowds gather in front of the Dakota, not sure who I was crying about.

When we bought the house the studio was just a decrepit shack at the back of the property with a sink, a toilet and a leaky roof. For years it was where we put things we didn't use anymore, like baby swings and three wheeled bikes; after Ted left and I banished every trace of him from the house in an orgy of redecorating, I fixed up the studio and turned it into a rental unit. The neighborhood isn't zoned for it, but I did it anyway—it's easier to say you're sorry later than ask permission first, and besides, I needed the money.

At first I only rented to gay men, who always improve property values and are more reliable than actors. Mostly they were thoughtful and kind, like Marc, who found a Wolf stove at a garage sale in Encino and dragged it home one day, and used to leave wonderful home-made challah on my doorstep every Friday. Patrick had planted and tended a beautiful rose trellis that was just coming into bloom. Jeffrey, who was an investigator in the D.A.'s office, once picked up Jessie at the police station and brought her home after she was arrested for shoplifting at Nordstrom's. It was one of Ted's weekends, the only time I felt free enough of my maternal responsibilities to do something you don't do when you're a single mother like go to Esalen and hang out naked in the baths, bring a man you've just met home for the night, or invite a group of your friends over while an earnest woman in a Che Guevara tee shirt and surgical pants who's doing outreach for the Women's

Clinic demonstrates how to use a handheld mirror and a speculum in order to get to know your own vagina. Ted happened to be playing golf that day, but Jeffrey was home, and when the police called I turned to him for help. Jessie spent the next three months of Saturdays cleaning restrooms in MacArthur Park, a diversion program for first-time offenders Jeffrey worked out with the juvenile court judge. Ted was royally pissed off, since he was all ready to challenge Nordstrom's right to arrest Jessie in the first place— something that seemed reasonable even to me, since she had three hundred dollars worth of cosmetics stuffed in her purse.

It was Jessie's only brush with the law. As far as I knew, the only illegal drug in the house was my own small stash of pot, which I hid so cleverly after I smoked it that I couldn't remember where it was the next time I wanted it. I'd never tried anything stronger than gin when the first man I slept with after Ted left offered me a joint: I don't know if Stan was, in fact, the greatest lover I ever had, but he remains that way in my mind. The memories of our lovemaking, even twenty five years later, still make me wet—while some women conjure up fantasies of sex with mysterious strangers or even movie stars, my imagination must be lacking, because it's Stan I feel inside me, his tongue, his fingers and long, skinny uncircumcised cock I imagine when I masturbate, which I do with the same regularity that I check my breasts, which is to say whenever I think of it, maybe once a month, and for similar reasons, which can be boiled down to use it or lose it.

I had my first real, scream-at-the-top-of-your-lungs, no-doubt-about-it orgasm with Stan. It was as if I'd suddenly been let in on a secret I didn't know was one; all those years with Ted and the few others before him, I thought I was getting steak, and it turned out it was only hamburger after all. How much of the ecstasy was due to Stan's considerable talents in the bedroom and how much to the dope still isn't clear, but sex never took me by surprise in quite the same way it did that first night in bed with him, and since pot is a lot easier to acquire these days than multiple orgasms, I've never entirely stopped using it.

The last man who rented the studio wasn't gay, and in time he became a lot more than a tenant, but not quite enough. John moved out a few months before I moved back to New York—the two situations weren't unrelated—and by then I didn't need the extra few hundred dollars a month, so I left it vacant. I store some clothes here I'd never wear in New York—for one thing, they're not black—and whenever I'm in L.A. to make the rounds or see the kids I stay here. But this time Jessie needed me, so I whistled Tory out of both our reveries, put the sunroof down on the Beemer, and headed into the setting sun.

By the time I arrived at Jessie's, she was in full Poor Me mode. True, the last couple of months of pregnancy aren't much fun—an alien being has taken over your body, your mind is all but gone and your moods are at the mercy of your hormones. But as I looked at my beautiful daughter in the full bloom of a much-desired pregnancy, being danced attendance upon by a husband she'd described to me even before I met him, as "every Jewish mother's wet dream," I felt more impatient than sympathetic.

Still, I flipped into mother mode, cooking and cleaning and running up and down stairs, bringing her meals and magazines and videos, giving her sponge baths and debating the merits of names I fervently hoped would slip her mind when the baby arrived (although "Hosannah," which I ridiculed when she first mentioned it, began to grow on me, which probably means I've already been in California too long).

I have been single for twice as long as I was married—still, living with Jessie and Zach was like watching an old movie, one I'd not only seen but also co-starred in in another lifetime. Had I been as cranky, querulous and demanding as Jessie when I was pregnant? Had Ted ever been as patient and understanding as Zach? Were we that scared, that brave, that young? And how did we end up so far from where we started? I silently implored my daughter to be nicer to her husband than she was, and the couple of times he snapped back at her I absented myself, taking Tory for a walk or closeting myself in my room. It would be the nursery when the baby came, but they hadn't gotten around to fixing it up yet; they were hoping to be out of the house by Jessie's due date, but even though they'd spent the last three months looking, they hadn't found anything they could afford.

"Unless I go back to work right away," Jessie told me. "Which I really don't want to do until the baby's at least two."

I knew this was my cue. I'd been generous with my kids—what was money for, if not to spend on the people you love?—and they had no reason to believe I wasn't as flush as I'd once been. Ted had anted up his half of their college tuitions, even though he got off cheap with Paul, and he'd ponied up for the extra hundred people Jessie invited to her wedding, which was only fair since most of them were his clients, which made at least part of his contribution, unlike any of mine, deductible. But it wouldn't occur to him to give Jessie and Zach the money for a down payment unless Jessie asked him directly, which Zach wouldn't let her do. He doesn't like Ted, and the feeling is mutual, which of course makes me love my son in law even more. Something happened between them soon after Ted's second divorce a couple of years ago—I don't know what it was, and neither Jessie or Zach has seen fit to enlighten me, despite my hinting around.

Instead of taking Jessie's bait about a house I volunteered to put up new wallpaper in the room—that was one of the few homemaking skills I'd learned at Frances's knee, and once Jessie chose one of the sample rolls I brought home, I got to work.

I'd forgotten what a smelly, backbreaking job it is, and by the time I finished I was exhausted. My back hurt, my arms felt like they weighed fifty pounds apiece, and it occurred to me that I probably ought to start taking the pills O'Neill had given me, except that I couldn't find them and the druggist at the pharmacy in Westwood next to my old gym, which had in fact been torn down and replaced with a new restaurant, refused to fill a prescription written by an out of state doctor.

On the way home from the drugstore, my cell phone rang.

"Sugar? Just a minute for Sandro, please," said Jeremy, his secretary, who kept me waiting for three red lights before putting Sandro through.

"Congratulations, sweetheart—they loved the script, they've green lighted the pilot!"

I was so delighted I let four cars cut into my lane ahead of me. "That's great news, Sandro—I'm thrilled!"

"They want a meeting tomorrow...can you make it? Sugar? You there?"

I was, but I had a funny feeling in my chest—was that my old pal the octopus again? "Yeah, I'm here...what time?" I rummaged around in my purse, found the nitro tablets, and slipped one under my tongue. It was probably a muscle spasm, I should have hired somebody to paper the nursery, but just in case ...and then the pressure eased up and went away.

"Ten in the morning, in Burbank—they'll leave a pass for you at the gate. You want to stop by here, we'll go together?"

"No, I'll meet you there. And Sandro...thanks."

"Wait 'till we get the deal signed. Then you can thank me. And Sugar..."

"Yes?"

"Behave yourself tomorrow. It's not a done deal yet."

CHAPTER
SIX

The surprise wasn't what Nelly Campbell, the head of network programming, said about the pilot—"It's perfect, we love it, it's all there"—or even what the handful of suits and assistant suits clustered around her glass and steel desk added—"Although we do have a couple of notes on the script." The surprise was walking into the meeting and finding Robin not only already there, but obviously very much at home.

"I'm so glad you could make it...Robin has been telling me all about you," said Nelly. She was one of those fit, nervous types common to the networks—body by Pilates, wardrobe by Stella McCartney, Botox and Restalyn by some Rumanian aesthetician on Melrose Avenue. "I had no idea you and she were partnering on the show."

"Neither did I," I managed to get out, shooting Sandro a look that said, What goes? He shook his head very slightly—not now, it signaled.

I'd been kicking the idea for the show around in my head for a while when I ran into Hedley Sturgis at a Ms. Foundation benefit. I'd known Hedley in L.A. when she was working with the Creative Coalition, which was just getting started then. She'd become a development exec in the network's New York office, and she called a few days after the benefit and invited me to lunch at Michael's. "What are you working on these days?" she asked over our Cobb salads, so I talked my idea up a little, and she expressed enough interest for me to go home that afternoon and put the beginnings of a pitch down on paper. Robin and I had become friends by then, and I brainstormed with her over a couple of meals before I sat down and wrote a treatment, which Hedley was high enough on to send to Nelly, who commissioned the pilot. I hadn't met Nelly before today, but since she was who I'd be dealing with, I'd come to the meeting prepared to make her my new best friend. Except that it looked like Robin had already beaten me to it.

I hadn't heard from Robin in a few days—actually, over a week, but I'd been so occupied with wallpapering the nursery and seeing to Jessie's needs that I hadn't noticed. "You know, I think I could eat something if you happen to be in the kitchen" had quickly become "Mom, I've been yelling for you for an hour, didn't you hear me?" and I wasn't sure what was going to give out first—my patience with my pregnant daughter or my walk-on in Echo Park as Mother Theresa.

Nelly caught the look Sandro shot me and passed the ball to a tall kid with a ponytail wearing leather jeans and a black tee shirt accessorized with a Mickey Mouse tie slung around his neck like the Red Baron. He stood up from his perch next to Robin on the arm of a curved, creamy suede sofa beneath the floor to ceiling windows in Nelly's light-filled corner office. "I think you know Kyle Ayrehart," Nelly said.

"Yeah, we met at that memorial thing for Jerry Orbach," he offered, reminding me why he looked so familiar. I wrote an episode of *Love, American Style* that Jerry guested way back when and we'd stayed in touch over the years. The service was top-heavy with celebrities as well as every actor who'd ever played a dead body on *Law and Order*, all working the room. Robin had exchanged air kisses with this kid and introduced us: "Kyle and I are old friends from Brown," she said, and after a tenth of a second of eye contact he looked over my head for someone more deserving of his attention. "He's in business development at ICM," she told me as he brushed past us; since that can mean anything from delivering the mail to doing deals, I didn't pay much attention.

As it turned out, I should have. "Kyle represents some talent we think might be right for the pilot," said Nelly.

"And Robin, of course," Kyle added.

She didn't look me directly in the eyes when Kyle said that, but she didn't seem embarrassed, either, just confident, like she owned the room, or at least had a second mortgage on it.

I was completely caught off guard. Why did Robin need an agent, and when had she become my partner? The show was my idea, the pilot was my creation, and what I'd paid her to do on it was work for hire—very well paid work, as a matter of fact.

"Yes, well, we'll have to work that out, won't we?" Sandro said to Kyle, and then, to Nelly, "I think this is great, just great, Sugar's going to bring this one home for you just like she did with *Going It Alone*, we can iron out the details later, but the first thing is, she'll take your notes and work them into the polish—what do you think, a week, ten days, Sugar? And we're already looking at the casting, we've got some great ideas, love to talk to you about them, Kyle, always glad to see you." And he hustled me out of Nelly's office before l could get in another word, which was probably a good idea, since the ones I was holding back began with "mother fucking" and ended with "cunt," which for my money is the worst thing you can call another woman, even if *Vagina Monologues* did give it a PC label.

Robin and Kyle stayed behind in Nelly's office while Sandro steered me down the hall and into the sunlight—I was disoriented, the way you are when you come out of the movies in the middle of the afternoon, surprised that it's still daylight. "Remember the one block rule," he warned, and even though I know better than to rehash a meeting or criticize a play or movie till you're out of hearing distance, I fumed silently until we got to a coffee shop far enough away from the danger zone so no one could eavesdrop on our conversation—not that anyone in the business would be caught dead there, it wasn't even a Starbuck's.

"What does Nelly mean, partnering with Robin? She's my fucking researcher, for Christ's sake! When did she acquire an agent? Doesn't that kid work in the mailroom? And what kind of notes are these, anyway?" I tossed the pages Nelly's assistant had handed me on my way out the door on the table after skimming the first couple of comments—the only thing that really registered were the neatly paired names on the oversized "From the desk of Nelly Campbell" Post-It slapped on the first one—"Kane/Westfield Script."

Maybe Robin had been more of my sounding board than my research assistant while I was writing the script and pulling together the show Bible—still, that was not only a long way from being my partner but so far from the truth I didn't know whether to laugh or cry. I couldn't believe she'd stabbed me in the back this way. That men can be sneaky and underhanded and craven isn't exactly news, but when a woman betrays you, it's different—it's like terrorism. Nothing prepares you for it, especially when it's someone you've done as much for as I'd done for her.

Here's the back story on Robin. Think willowy, blonde, porcelain-skinned, southern, and smart—Diane Sawyer, but younger and taller, with the same knack for hiding her keen intelligence behind her baby blues so it doesn't put people off. She has pretty impressive credentials –an apple blossom princess and a mainstay of the Winchester Hunt, a Madeira deb who finished cum laude at Brown and topped that off with the Radcliffe publishing course.

When I met her she was laboring for slave wages at Doubleday, which loaned her to me to do the fact checking, photo permissions, copyediting and interview transcribing for *Love, Lexy*—all the shit work of pulling together a celebrity bio. When the book was done, she quit the publishing house and pieced together a career doing the same kind of things for other writers, plus a couple of short-term projects at Conde Nast, which likes its young things not only quick and well-connected but also thin and fashionable enough to grace its stylish halls. I knew she'd been working on a novel, too; I'd wondered if it was one of those *romans a clef* that hangs all the author's former employers' dirty laundry out to dry in the public eye. "Do you think if she ever gets it published, there'll be some grotesque caricature of me in it?" I asked Carrie.

"Don't worry, you're not famous enough, and besides, she's got bigger fish to fry," Carrie replied. She's never been a big fan of Robin's, for reasons I put down to her working class origins which express themselves in her innate dislike of the privileged class; Robin, who spends summer weekends at her parents' "cottage" in Amagansett and winters at their houses in Aspen and St. Bart's, is a card-carrying member.

I'd hired Robin to research the arcane details of how detective agencies actually work and pull together some stuff for me on art theft and forgery, which was what set the story in motion. She got a nice bonus out of the deal; she met a good looking cop on the art theft squad, a change from the masters of the universe she generally favors—the last I' d heard, the romance was still going strong.

I'd paid her twice the going rate for what she did for me—mostly editing and typing, although since Robin and Clea, the second lead in the show, are about the same age it was useful to have someone helping me out with Clea's cultural references and style icons. Jessie's that generation, too, and could probably fill me in on what they listen to and the labels they prize, but these days she's more into Mozart for Mommies-to-Be and her style is mostly Belly Basics, so I made do with Robin.

I'd also used a few of her ideas in the bible, which is the big book for a TV series. The bible has all the details on the setting, the characters and their histories; it's what the writing team uses so they can get inside your head without you having to tell them everything. The bible is even more important than the script itself. The characters have to be distinct enough to register, but not so obviously cloned from life that the show won't work if you don't get exactly the talent you have in mind, so while Amelia's description might fit

Candice Bergen to a tee, it would also work for a lot of other actresses her age (and God knows there are plenty to choose from). Along with the script and the bible, I'd outlined half a dozen episodes, but I didn't expect to write them all. There were a couple of writers whose scripts for *Arrested Development* and *Desperate Housewives* had caught my eye, and along with Nelly's notes there were some network-acceptables she'd suggested. Of course, no offers would be made until we were further along in the process. First I had to turn in a finished shooting script, then we'd cast the pilot, and then, if the network picked it up, we'd put together a writing team.

Robin wasn't ready for a place on the team yet, but she was clever and original, and one of her ideas for an episode was so good I'd planned to try her out on it, since according to Guild rules, you have to give one episode a season to a freelancer, even if you don't use it—it's a kind of union featherbedding, the throwaway, but sometimes you actually get something wonderful, and the writer may even make it onto the team. And even if it's not right for your show, whoever does it ends up with a little money and a spec script they can use to pitch somewhere else.

"Will you tell me what the hell went on in there?" I asked Sandro. "Who was that masked man, anyway? I thought he was a kid in the mailroom at ICM."

"Not anymore," said Sandro. "He's the hot new boy at UTA and he reps that girl on *The L Word*—the slutty one. From what Robin was saying before you came in, they think she'd be perfect for Clea."

"Who's 'they?' And what the fuck was Robin doing there, anyway?"

"According to Jeremy she's been out here for a week, talking up the show like it's her baby." Jeremy is Sandro's pipeline to the dish on the up and coming kids in the industry. "Apparently, she and Kyle slipped Nelly a few notes of their own, including making his client the lead. And they suggested a few other changes, too—here."

He handed me a blue UTA binder with "Kyle Ayrehart" in little gold letters in the lower left hand corner. Inside was a "Dear Nell" letter—"Here are some possibilities you might want to consider for the pilot," with a list of names and a handful of headshots. Another page was titled "Some Things to Think About," which began "With Clea as the lead, we reach the all-important 18–34 market..."

I kept reading, dumbfounded. Amelia had been reduced to a ghostly presence—and not metaphorically, either. In Kyle's notes she is dispatched violently at the end of the first episode and hangs around in future ones, giving her daughter motherly advice, like telling her to do something with her hair and warning her not to sleep with the suave, dashing thief, described as a young Bruce Willis—"Do I have to tell you who represents him?" Sandro asked.

"Why do I feel like it's the *Twilight Zone* and I've just turned into Margo Channing in a remake of *All About Eve*?" I replied. "Who does this little *pisher* think he is? Excuse me, these two *pishers*."

"Look, Sugar, if it were up to me, I'd tell that jerk to go fuck himself... all those jerks. But she got the first fuck in, your little pal Robin."

"You mean literally? She slept with that kid in the dirty T-shirt?"

"I don't know if she shtupped him or not. The thing is, she screwed you. Big time. Nelly's nuts about her. "

"What can I do?"

"Well, the contract calls for one rewrite and one polish. You know, it doesn't matter who wrote the original script, even if that's the one they green lighted, which it is in this case. But from here on, what matters is who writes the one they shoot. So you better get your ass in gear, that's all I can say. Of course, if you use any of Robin's ideas, we'll have to give her a credit."

"And if I don't?"

He shrugged. "Let me feel Nelly out. If Kyle's sold her on going younger, you may have to."

"I'm not killing Amelia off!" I said hotly.

"Nobody said you should," he said soothingly. "Look, Nelly knows what's going on—she told me she had a long talk with Hedley before the meeting today. But she also said it might not be a bad idea for you to work with someone who's tuned into what younger women are like these days, and since Robin's already involved..."

"I'm not working with that back-stabbing little bitch! I'd rather take the script somewhere else!"

"You know we can't do that, honey...Nelly owns the first draft. You polish up the pilot, and if it goes, then I'll see what I can work out. But if it goes to series, I think you and Robin are going to have to kiss and make up."

CHAPTER
SEVEN

Jessie and I were both due at the end of the month, and it was a race to see which of us finished first.

She was as bored with bed rest as she was when she was six years old and had the measles, but I didn't have the time or patience to entertain her the way I did then. I knew she was scared about the birth itself—what first-time mother isn't?—and naturally I told her the Big Lie about forgetting how much it hurt once you hold your baby in your arms. So did her girlfriends, who came to visit with their babies and regaled her with minute by minute accounts of their own experience, from the first Braxton Hicks to the final triumphant push—apparently they'd all won the natural childbirth Olympics except one, who said with a wisdom beyond her years, "I expect I'll suffer enough for the next eighteen years, why start at the beginning?" And they all toted thousands of dollars of mother and baby accessories—I'd drop the names, but do you really care about this season's status pram? Jessie did, though, and the stuff she ordered every day on-line or sent me to pick up overflowed the nursery, which was beginning to look like the stock room at Babies R Us.

When she wasn't worrying about labor and delivery she obsessed about the most statistically improbable things that could already be wrong with the baby. "Has anyone in our family ever had coloboma?" she wanted to know.

"I had an Argentinian once, but a Colombian, no I don't think so," I said.

"Oh, Mother, I said coloboma. It's what happens when the baby's eyes don't finish developing."

"Don't worry, Joey doesn't have Colombia." We didn't know the baby's gender, but we'd taken to calling him that after he jumped hard enough to upset the Scrabble board on Jessie's stomach right after I used the "j" for a 30-point triple.

She worried about anything she might have done to harm the baby, like the X-rays the dentist took before she knew she was pregnant and something the pharmacist in Cancun gave her for *turista* when they went there to celebrate after she found out. "Aren't you jumping the gun a little?" I asked. "Mother guilt doesn't come in until your milk does. Besides, I did everything you're not supposed to do now—coffee, cigarettes, alcohol—and you turned out fine."

"So far," she said darkly. "Some prenatal effects don't show up for years."

"You should get rid of her copy of *What to Expect When You're Expecting,*" said Hallie. We were standing in the shallow end of her swimming pool, pushing her grandson Max around in his floatee, which looked like a little tugboat and had a striped awning to protect him from the sun. "I read it when Amanda was carrying Max. All the things that book warns you could happen, if you read it first, you'd never get pregnant...and then where would *you* be, my precious darling, huh? Where would Maxie be?" She whirled the baby around in a circle, which made him laugh with glee and reach his chubby little arms up to her. "You think you loved your kids unconditionally, but when you have one of these you realize you didn't, not the way you love your grandchildren. They don't have to *do* anything to get it, they just have to *be*...isn't that right, Maxie? Just be? Do bee do bee do...whee! Just wait, you'll see."

"Believe me, I'm more than ready," I sighed.

"What's going on? You look a little ragged around the edges."

"I forgot how much work it is to get a show on the air. The last time I did it I was a lot younger."

Hallie nodded sympathetically. "At a certain point in life we're too old for some things, like camping out on the ground or learning a foreign language."

"Or pulling all nighters. Even if my back could take it, my brain doesn't function at three in the morning any more."

When the kids were growing up, I wrote mostly at night, loving the quiet that settled over the house when they were asleep and I knew I wouldn't be interrupted in the middle of a thought or a sentence. I'd hear them stir in the morning and then I'd stop and do the mother thing—make breakfast and lunches and check their homework, brush the tangles out of Jessie's hair and find Paul's soccer shoes. I'd drive them to school or walk them to the bus stop, still in my old sweats, and then come home and collapse until it was time to pick them up. It was years since I'd done that, but every time I took out my laptop at Jessie's and tried to work, she needed something, and by the time Zach came home I didn't have the energy.

I was still on the day shift in Echo Park. I'd arrive there before Zach left for the restaurant in the morning, and stay until he came home unless Jessie had company and didn't need me. But I'd moved my toothbrush, dog and laptop back to Laurel Canyon. When you've lived alone as long as I have, it's hard to adjust to the rhythms of other people's lives, and I've never really been able to write anywhere except in my own surroundings. But when even that didn't get my creative juices flowing, I hung out with Hallie.

We've known each other since our kids were in kindergarten together; she's the friend I miss most when I'm not here and can't wait to see again when I come back. We're still on each other's wavelength and speed dial, even though for the last few years we haven't been in the same time zone very often.

Hallie is a queen among the queen bees of L.A. real estate, a far cry from the Montana girl who came out here on the back of Peter Fonda's

Harley, or maybe it was one of the Bridges boys, back in the day when all those brilliant young actors hung around Livingston or Missoula shooting and screwing and drinking and drugging between movies until the ones who'd been nerds in high school, like George Lucas and Steven Spielberg, replaced them with mechanical sharks and ray guns and ushered in the era of the blockbuster. Between then and now, Hallie's stayed happily married to a short sweet *shmata* manufacturer whose idea of a hot time is two scotches before dinner with his sexy, statuesque, redheaded wife, who he calls his *shiksa* cowgirl.

"So how are things with you?" I asked after we'd put Max down for a nap in the shade and stretched out on the lounge chairs with gin and tonics and cheese and crackers.

"About the same, minus the details." With really good friends, the ones whose hearts you can see into, the shorthand is enough. Better, the same, worse—you know what it means without asking, so you don't. Instead you reach across the space between you and squeeze her hand, and she knows you know, and she's glad she doesn't have to explain it any better than that.

Somehow, on the way to the perfect life we feel entitled to for our children—the life we secretly believe they owe us—Hallie's daughter had picked up a heroin habit, which was why Hallie was playing with her grandson on a sunny weekday afternoon when she might otherwise have been showing a newly anointed studio head or expatriate Iranian currency trader a ten million dollar fixer-upper in the flats of Beverly or a ten thousand square foot Tudor in Holmbly Hills. Heroin is one of those words like "terminal" you can't imagine hearing in connection with your kid—it's not even on the list of things you worry about, especially when, like Amanda, they sail through high school and college and marry a sweet guy who gives them a nice home and a beautiful little boy.

The sweet guy had divorced Amanda and won custody of Max—"I don't blame him, if he were my son, I'd have told him to do the same thing," Hallie said sadly. There wasn't much she could do for Amanda except pay for another stint in rehab, but Max needed her, and his father was grateful for her help.

About a week after I got out here Hallie had a dinner party for me... old friends, people we'd both known for years, through marriages, births, divorces, deaths, remarriages, cross-country moves—all the rituals of our lives. The conversation turned to our kids, the way it always does, and when it got around to Hallie she went on and on about Amanda's sister, Sarah, who'd just finished a Ph.D. in environmental studies at Berkeley and won an NSF grant to study mushroom spores in Peru.

"That's what you do," she said later, after everyone left and she gave me the real low-down—the producer whose kid who turned their cabin in Big Bear into a meth lab, the broker whose son was doing time for kiting checks, the plastic surgeon whose daughter's boyfriend had put her in the hospital twice but still refused to leave him. "You talk about the one who's doing fine, or you brag or you lie—sometimes both at the same time. Because telling the truth—that you're scared or frightened or furious or frustrated about your kids, that you're disappointed in how they turned out, is just too embarrassing. And you know the worst part, the dirtiest little secret? It's how much you envy the ones whose kids are great, not even stars, not fabulously rich or accomplished, but just okay." Her torrent of words slowed down. "Not you," she said. "I'm glad yours are fine, I didn't mean you, I meant people like Georgia, whose kid just made his fifth million, and Laurie, whose daughter wrote that best-seller."

"Tell you what, when one of mine wins a MacArthur or finds a cure for cancer, you can envy me to your heart's content," I said.

"Deal," she agreed, and we had another gin and tonic before I went back to my studio and tried to work.

Every writer I know has a different set of rituals to get the creative juices flowing, a different combination of space, place and atmosphere. For a long time now mine have required a city where you can order in your life, from coffee and newspapers to new sweats from the Gap to replace the ones that would walk away by themselves if you ever took them off to wash them, which you don't—I don't, anyway—when you're facing a deadline. I was used to being someplace where when you get tired of listening to yourself think but don't really want to talk to anybody, you can take an elevator down to the street and be in a crowd of people who give you the feeing that you're still part of the human race, or conduct small commercial transactions with familiar strangers, like the guy at the newsstand who knows you want Marlboro Lites as well as the new *Time Out* or the woman at the dry cleaner's who doesn't complain when you've lost your ticket. An errand like that, maybe a peek into Filene's or Nine West—when you come back, sometimes the problem's solved itself.

Out here, though, you have to drive to get anywhere, and it's a whole big *megillah*, so swimming would have to do. I don't know where my mind goes when I swim laps, but sometimes afterward, when it comes back from wherever it's been, it works better. I fiddled around with the script for a couple of unproductive hours before I packed it in and went next door to the Jameson's pool; they'd given me a key to the gate years ago and told me to treat it like my own, and since they're hardly ever home, I do. Maybe a few laps would wake up the right side of my brain.

I was trying to build up Clea's role without relegating Amelia to the occasional walk-on—like Stockard Channing on the *West Wing*—and create a love interest, because the one thing all the suits agreed on was that *Discretion Advised* was "lacking sexual tension." Actually, that was the second thing—they hated that name, too. I wasn't particularly attached to it either, but you can drain all the air out of a promising idea while you wait for the right handle, and I knew it would come to me in time...maybe even in the pool. A little pot might nudge things along, but I didn't have any, because since 9-11 it's a bad idea to travel with even one little joint tucked between your bra and the under side of your breast, the way I used to. They're patting down all kinds of people in order to prove they're not profiling certain ones—it would be just my luck to run into some TSA type who got his kicks from feeling up women old enough to be his mother. In New York I buy pot at a bodega a couple of blocks from my apartment, but I had no idea where to get it here any more.

I hadn't missed it in the weeks I'd been in California. Or cigarettes, either, except for the one at night, before I went to sleep—the smell made Jessie nauseous, and even second hand smoke was apparently worse than thalidomide for a fetus. I'd lost a little weight, too, a result of reacquainting myself with the kitchen and cooking meals for Jessie that had little to recommend them except what they didn't have—sugar, salt, or fat. Sometimes Zach brought dessert home from the restaurant, and a couple of times I gave into a midnight craving for a Pink's chili dog, but between the stairs in their house, the laps in the Jameson's pool, and my daily walks with Tory when Jessie was resting, I was putting out more calories than I took in.

Without really intending to—almost in spite of myself, which is pretty stupid when you think about it—I was taking better care of myself than I usually did. When I got back to New York, I'd impress O'Neill with the new, healthy me.

Sandro called me almost every day. "Getting anywhere with the rewrite?"

"Not so you'd notice it."

"Have you heard from Robin?"

"Not really." She'd phoned twice, leaving an 818 number, but I hadn't returned her calls.

"You've got to get past this, Sugar. At least have lunch with her. See what she's got to say for herself. Maybe you can find a way to work it out. Nelly's very concerned."

If I'd been on a roll I wouldn't have bothered, but unless I could manage to bring the pilot in by myself, which wasn't happening, I had to. I needed her. Even more, I wanted—no, needed—an explanation for why she'd tried to fuck me over, just in case she had one. It's like hoping a man will tell you a lie you can make yourself believe, even when a woman answers the phone in his hotel room or you find lipstick on his shorts.

"I'll talk to Kyle—we'll do a little *hondling,* give her a credit, a little money, maybe put her on the writing team," said Sandro. "The important thing is Nelly wants her, she thinks she'll be good for the script, good to backstop you if it gets picked up."

"What do you mean, backstop me?"

"I don't have to tell you, being a show runner's plenty tough, you want someone around to do the heavy lifting. But we're not going to get to that stage, not if you don't give Nelly what she wants, and...."

"And what she wants is Robin, right?"

"It wouldn't hurt."

CHAPTER
EIGHT

"I don't think this relationship is working," said Robin.

"My sentiments exactly," I replied.

Sandro had set up the meeting because every time I picked up the phone to do it myself I got mad all over again. I still didn't want to talk to her, but he'd made it clear that as far as Nelly was concerned, that wasn't an option. "She's not saying you have to bring her on as a co-writer," he told me. "Just that she has some good ideas, and you ought to listen. So go and make nice and then we'll figure out a way to buy her off."

"Blow her off is more like it. I've already paid her. And pretty generously, I might add," I protested.

"Sweetheart, just relax and let me take care of it. That's what you pay me the big bucks for. The important thing is, you get the script done. So far it's a one-off. If Nelly's not happy with the product, she won't green light the pilot. And she won't be happy with it unless you put Robin on the team."

"What's with that? Robin's not sleeping with Nelly, is she?"

"It's the goniff with the ponytail she's sleeping with. And he just happens to be Nelly's college roommate's stepson's best friend or something like that. The point is, you need Nelly. And if she says you need Robin, then you need her, too."

I hate needing. It's my least favorite thing to feel. Wanting—that's different. Wanting is what makes the world go around, it gets you out of bed in the morning. But needing is the pits.

I threaded my way through traffic on Pico, trying out a few opening lines that would convey just how angry and betrayed I felt while still leaving my dignity intact. I hadn't come up with any when I handed my car over to the valet at Shutters and made my way to Pedals, the café on the bike path, narrowly avoiding a collision with a woman on inline skates pushing a baby jogger.

Robin was already seated when I arrived, flirting prettily with a good-looking waiter who hovered attentively over her. She was dressed in what passes for business casual in LA—white linen walking shorts, a gauzy print camisole, and a beautifully cut black blazer that screamed Armani. We exchanged the obligatory compliments about how good we both looked—at least I was telling the truth—and then she relieved me of the responsibility of getting the first word in by saying precisely what I was thinking.

"We don't really understand the dynamic between these two women," she added, and I missed a couple of beats before I realized she was talking about Amelia and Clea, not her and me.

"What's to understand? They're mother and daughter."

"Yes, but, where is it written that they have to be?"

"On pages 1 to 95. Not to mention the bible. Look, Robin, I don't know what you're trying to do here, but—"

She looked at me evenly. "I'm trying to help," she said.

"You certainly have an interesting way of going about it. Taking a script that someone else wrote—using my name, my reputation, and my work—to get what? Money? An agent? A credit? A deal?" I caught the waiter's eye. "I've changed my mind, I think I will have a drink after all—a bloody Mary, please."

"All I want is to help you get your show on the air. That's all I've ever wanted," she replied defensively.

"I'm glad you understand that—that it's *my* show. As for wanting to help—don't you think you might have asked me before you and whatshisname –"

"—Kyle"

"—before you and Kyle teamed up and sandbagged me with Nelly and the network?"

"That's not what happened. We didn't plan it that way. At least I didn't," said Robin.

"Really? Then just how did it happen?"

"Kyle read the script and thought his new client would be great for Clea."

"You showed it to him without my permission?"

"Not exactly. It was on my night table and he picked it up and skimmed through it while I was in the shower."

"I see." I wondered how long they'd been fucking each other before they decided to fuck me, and just who was using whom.

"Look, he already knew it was in development at the network—he saw it in the trades, just like everybody else. Remember when all those AD's and writers called you after that item ran in *Variety*? What's the difference?"

"The difference is, nothing's final yet. We don't have a go. And we haven't put it out for casting."

"So? When did that ever stop an agent from trying to get a client in early?"

"And which client would that be, Robin? You? Or that girl from *The L Word*?"

"Her. At least, at first."

"And now?"

She sighed. "Look, Sugar, I never made any secret of the fact that I don't want to be a glorified researcher forever. Publishing is dead. The pay is awful. And I've been thinking about moving out here. A lot of my friends have left New York since 9-11. Besides, Kyle and I—you've had a few long-distance relationships yourself. You know they never seem to work."

"It's gotten to that point, huh?"

"We've been seeing each other for a few months, since that memorial service. Obviously, he can't leave L.A. And if the show goes…well, I was hoping there'd be something for me in it."

"I was, too, Robin. In fact, I'd planned to ask you if you wanted to be involved. But that's a long way from this hostile takeover you and Kyle have dreamed up. Not to mention turning my script into *Moonlighting* meets the *Ghost and Mrs. Muir*!"

"It wasn't that way, Sugar—really, it wasn't. As a matter of fact, I thought that was a terrible idea. Amelia's a great character. But Clea—she's still pretty unformed. There's not much back-story on her…even Nelly brought that up. She thinks she's underwritten. Like, what's her motivation? Why does she work for Amelia? She's smart, she's a genius with computers, she could get a job anywhere, so why isn't she more independent? Why is she still under her mother's thumb? You don't see Alexa Stewart working for her mother, do you? And Amelia's almost as controlling as Martha. If you want the younger demographic, you've got to make Clea a more interesting character. More like Jennifer Lee Hewitt in that movie with Sigourney Weaver and less like the *Gilmore Girls*. You've written her like a grown-up version of the daughter in *Going It Alone*—or like you and Jessie."

She was right, and her points were valid. I'd written Amelia's back story pretty thoroughly, but I still hadn't dug into Clea.

"I was thinking—this is just an idea—what if it's Clea who talks her way into the chateau and verifies that the stolen Vermeer is there instead of Amelia? And what if it's Clea and Amelia together who convince Jean Paul to pull off one last job and steal it back? They can't seduce him—Amelia's too old and Clea's too obvious. But if they play off each other—Amelia trying to charm him into it, Clea challenging and dismissive—forget it, Mother, I told you he was over the hill, he's lost his nerve, we're wasting our time, that kind of thing —that could work."

I was sifting through the possibilities while Robin raced ahead.

"Maybe that's Clea's back story—she's always wanted to be an actress, and Amelia never wanted her to be, there's the conflict; it's totally understandable, what mother would? She's always going out on auditions but she never gets anywhere, but she sees this chance to show Amelia she can act, so—"

"...she poses as the night nurse or the gardener's daughter or something and comes back with a photo of the painting while Amelia's still trying to figure out how to set it up—"

"Right! The point is, she's not just window dressing, Amelia needs her—"

"But she doesn't want to put her in danger, she's her daughter..."

"True, but she's a lot more competent than Amelia thinks she is, gutsier, riskier. Their relationship is more balanced this way—there are more possibilities in it, especially in the other episodes. Like the one where Amelia has to find a new kidney for the sick child, but the sperm bank won't tell the mother who the donor was—"

"She could get in there as a potential client and get access to the files—"

"...and in the missing microchip case, she could be—"

"...the one who does the handover after the money's been paid-"

"...after they *think* it's been paid..."

I was feeling the way I do when the juice starts flowing—suddenly the script was alive with possibilities again, the pieces coming together in my mind. I wasn't a hundred percent sold on any of the ideas Robin had floated, but the give and take reminded me that having someone to bounce ideas off of was what I'd been missing.

In the show bible, which wasn't yet much more than an outline, I hadn't filled in all the detail I'd need if the pilot went to series. I knew Amelia— she was a woman of a certain age, which in Hollywood is any female over 35, clever, charming, seductive, and still sexy enough to appeal to men, although if she ever actually sleeps with one it's not spelled out in the script—I could just imagine the hoots of disbelief if I suggested that a mature woman actually has sex. Amelia took over the agency after her husband died, and created it in her own image; no scruffy ex-cops peeping Motel 6's to catch philandering spouses in the act, just well-heeled, well-connected clients who were missing something they needed her to get back.

"I had an idea about the title..." Robin stopped and looked at me hesitantly. Oh well, in for a penny...

"*Finders Keepers*," she pronounced.

"Not bad, but she doesn't keep what she retrieves, just a percentage of what it's worth—"

"*Finders Fee?*"

"That's better but it's still not it. Let's leave that for later and concentrate on the other stuff in Nelly's notes"

I didn't realize how much time had passed until the waiter tactfully reminded us that they were about to set up for dinner.

"So where do we go from here?" Robin asked.

"I don't know," I replied truthfully. "Today was fun. I'm uh, grateful for your contributions. I just don't like having them forced on me."

"You don't have to use them," she pointed out. "You could always tell Nelly you thought them up yourself."

Sure I could, if I didn't mind covering all the mirrors in my house.

"Look, why don't we just let Sandro and Kyle work it out, okay? They know the Guild regs better than we do. I'm not trying to screw you out of anything."

"I'm not, either. I just wanted a chance to show you what I could do, that's all. I'm not a writer, I know that...I junked the novel, by the way, it was terrible. But there are other ways I could be involved. If you let me."

I wasn't quite ready to let her off the hook.

"I don't have much of a choice, do I?"

She wasn't, either. "I guess that's up to you."

CHAPTER
NINE

"Which one is yours?"

I was standing in front of the nursery window, checking out the Most Beautiful Baby competition—not that there was any, of course. I would have told Jessie her daughter was gorgeous even if she looked like Winston Churchill, but when I held Rosie in my arms for the first time, it was clear I wouldn't have to; she was exquisite, from the feathery tendrils of soft dark hair that curled around her pale, heart-shaped face to the perfectly formed toenails on her tiny little feet.

"The second one from the left," I said.

"Oh, the beautiful one," he replied knowingly.

"I bet you say that to... all of us." I'd started to say, to all the grandmas, but something stopped me. It's been a while since I really noticed a man, forever since I did that thing you do when you meet an attractive one and wonder what it would be like to fuck him.

He wasn't movie star handsome, but he had a comfortable, weathered, lived-in face, saved from unremarkableness by a pair of truly arresting eyes. I have only seen eyes that color on Elizabeth Taylor, whom I once encountered in the ladies lounge at Saks. They didn't look like colored contacts, thank God—I know it's sexist, but vanity is so much more forgivable in a woman, isn't it? And besides, he was looking at me with the kind of frank, appraising interest no man had directed my way in so long I almost turned around to see if there was someone standing behind me.

Back in the eighties when the *Times* was still publishing that "About Men" column in the Sunday magazine, which Abe Rosenthal started to show that women weren't the only ones with feelings, they ran an essay about how invisible we are to them once we're past a certain age, once our looks or sex appeal or aura of possibility no longer interests them. When they pass us on the street or stand next to us in an elevator or glance at us even momentarily, they don't really see us—we simply don't register in their awareness. That was the set-up for the piece, before the writer got to the topic sentence; recently he'd realized that the same thing had begun to happen to him. Women— particularly young, desirable women—were looking right through or past him, not even noticing that he existed.

I couldn't muster one whit of empathy for him, just a gleeful, venial delight—I was over thirty then, and already knew that in a few years I'd be invisible, too. But at least it wouldn't surprise me.

"Which one is yours?" I asked.

"None of them," he replied. "I just like looking at them. Thinking about all the beginnings, the possibilities, and the potential. Who they'll be, what will happen to them."

"Really?"

He was even better looking when he smiled. He was wearing a soft blue work shirt tucked into faded jeans, and his stubble was more salt than pepper. He could be a working class guy who'd just forgotten to shave for a couple of days, but I didn't think so; his voice was educated and his shoes looked expensive.

"See that one waving his arm around, with those big shoulders? Maybe he'll win the Heisman Trophy in twenty years or so. And that one over there with the spit curl and squint and that prim little mouth—"

"The one who looks like Condoleeza Rice?"

"I was thinking about a school teacher but you're right, there's a definite resemblance."

We speculated about the other babies—"A concert pianist, that one, look at those hands—"A politician, he's smiling already"—and then I said, "Come here often?" I wasn't flirting, not really...unless he was.

"Isn't that my line?" Yes, he was. Be still my heart—you've just become a grandmother, for God's sake.

Just then Jessie padded down the hall. "Dr. Levine was just in, he said we can go, so Zach's packing up the room and I'm going to feed her before we leave. Are you coming with us?"

"No, I have to let Tory out of the car, she's been cooped up for hours. And I've got some things to do. I'll come by later." After a five-hour labor, Rosie had arrived with a lusty squall a little late the previous night; when her mother was born I stayed in the hospital for almost a week, but these days drive-by deliveries are the norm.

"Okay," she said, opening the door to the nursery. I watched as she settled into a wooden rocking chair and nestled Rosie against her breast, very conscious of the man standing next to me. Then I blew my two babies a kiss and turned to leave.

He walked alongside me down the corridor and followed me into the elevator. "It's too early for dinner and too late for lunch, and you don't even know me, but there's a Peet's cart out back near the doctor's parking lot and their coffee's a lot better than the cafeteria. How about it?"

The elevator stopped on the first floor, and he steered me past the information desk and the front lobby and down a hall that terminated in an exit door marked "Staff Only" on the side facing the lot.

"You seem to know your way around here," I said, hurrying to keep up with his long strides. "Are you a doctor?"

"No," he said. "I'm in biotechnology."

"So you're here on business?"

"You could say that," he replied. "But a little while ago it got to be pleasure."

It might have been a hot flash, or maybe it was sunstroke, but I could feel myself blushing.

"I'm Alex—Alex Carroll," he said.

"Charlotte Kane," I replied, "but most people call me Sugar."

When he grinned he looked ten years younger, but I thought he was around my age, give or take a few years. Despite the faint drawl in his voice, he was from Seattle; he said he'd lived in Texas for a long time. "I had a small biotech company in Austin, and when Immunex acquired it they got me, too. I moved up there a few years ago, worked out my contract, and left."

"And now?"

"Another start-up—once you've done it, you're never happy working for somebody else. What about you?"

"I'm in television, which is all about working for a lot of somebody elses." I hadn't heard from Sandro since turning in the rewrite, and now that the baby was safely here, I was starting to worry again.

"Don't play well with others, huh?"

"*Some* others," I said, and he grinned again.

We drank our coffee and did that feeling-out thing where you give each other carefully edited bits of your story and try to figure out who the stranger you're talking to is, once you're sure he's not a serial killer or a Scientologist. He walked me to my car and won extra points for recognizing Tory's breed.

"Most people think she's a poodle," I said as she sniffed the median parking strip and then squatted in relief.

"I've had a couple of Porties," he said. "One of them lived to be fifteen, then we got another one. They're great dogs."

"Where's the other one?"

"In Houston," he said. I'd noticed he wasn't wearing a wedding ring, but that doesn't tell you much. "My ex got custody."

I took Tory's dish and a liter of bottled water out of the trunk and we made small talk while she drank and peed again, agreeing that the Getty was great architecture but had lousy art, that Joan Didion got California better than any writer since Nathaniel West, that if George Bush would only do his wife instead of doing the country, not to mention the world, we'd feel a lot safer. We disagreed about whether universal medical care was a right, not a privilege, if rap music should be broadcast on a frequency only people under 21could hear, and whether if you were Chinese and ate it three times a day you'd still love Chinese food. He seemed to enjoy a lot of things that scared me like scuba diving, heliskiing, and mountain climbing; I used my O'Neill lines about jumping to conclusions and running off at the mouth, which got a much better reaction from him than they had in the hospital.

Tory began to pant—it was hot out there in the parking lot—and I could feel what little reserve of energy I had draining away. Alex Carroll seemed to realize that; "Long day, I guess," he said, and I nodded.

"I've been at the hospital half of last night and all day today," I said. "I really need to go home."

I'd already decided that if he asked for my number, I'd give it to him—not that that meant anything more than "Let's have lunch," but there was a definite current between us, unless I was the only one who felt it. And even if I wasn't, I'm still not comfortable doing the asking.

He was, though. "Will you have dinner with me tomorrow night?"

"I'd like that," I said.

"Me too," he replied. We made a plan to talk the next afternoon and I drove off, wondering if he'd really call me. Just in case, I made an appointment with Douglas at Umberto's for a haircut and with Roxanne for a manicure, although I passed on the bikini wax; there's hardly enough there to justify either the price or the pain. I was amazed when Jessie told me a few years ago—before she got married—that she waxed twice a month. "Men expect it," she said. "They won't go down on you if you have a hairy pussy."

When the girls heard that, they were as stunned as I was. Carrie said, "When we stopped shaving our pits, let alone our legs, it was a political act. Don't they realize that having your pubic hair pulled out to please a man is one, too?"

Traffic on the 405 was sluggish so I returned all my phone calls—I'd made the most important ones from the hospital, Frances first and then Paul, who said he'd had a feeling Jessie was in labor, he'd been waiting to hear the good news. I left messages for Carrie and Peggy and Suzanne and Hallie, who phoned me back just as the cars ahead of me started to move. "Six feet, 175 pounds and gorgeous," I told her.

"The baby?"

"No, this incredible guy who picked me up in the hospital." I was just getting down to the specifics—that great smile and the midnight blue eyes that were practically purple—when my cell did its call waiting thing. "Call you back, it's my agent," I said.

"You go, grandma!" she replied, and according to Sandro, this was just what this one was doing.

"It's a green light, for sure this time," he said. "Nelly loved the rewrite, it's a go, signed on the dotted line. They're not even asking for a polish—said as soon as we get a director, we can go right to shooting script."

"That's fantastic!" I said.

"Not entirely," he replied. "It's still a one-off—they won't make any decision about a series 'till they see how the pilot goes. And they want it fast—shooting will start in April in Vancouver, and you have to bring it in in 28 days. So you've really got to move on this, Sugar—you've got to get a director, a bunch of AD's, a cast, a production designer...you know the drill. You sure you're up for this?

"Well of course I am, what makes you think I'm not? I've done this before, you know, I'm not exactly a newbie."

"Of course you're not, sweetheart. By the way, congratulations on the baby. I can't believe little Jessie, all grown up, a kid of her own now...seems like yesterday she was hanging around the set of *Going It Alone* in pigtails. And now you're a *bubbe*!"

"Thanks for the little stroll down memory lane, Sandro. What is it? You think I'm too old to pull this off? Does Nelly?"

He backtracked and sweet-talked, sounding as sincere as a car salesman while I half-listened, running my tongue around my teeth, searching for the site of the pain that had been nagging at me for days now—damn, it hurt somewhere in there, I just didn't know where. My old dentist had retired— I'd have to ask Zach's mother for the name of hers. Stacy is one of those women who treat you to an organ recital every time you ask how she is, but she's information central when it comes to medical professionals, and the fact that her son isn't one is the great tragedy of her life. When I met Zach's parents for the first time, Stacy raved about Jessie—"So beautiful! So smart! So ambitious, we couldn't be happier!" And then she added, only slightly apologetically, "I'm sure you wanted a doctor for her, or at least a lawyer."

Poor Zach, I'd thought, and still do. "I'd always rather eat than get sick or sue someone, and so would Jessie," I told her. "I am totally nuts about Zach, and besides, I'll never have to cook a Thanksgiving turkey again."

"Sugar, you there?" Sandro asked.

"Yes, I'm here. What were you saying?"

"They've assigned a producing team already—the guys we met in Nelly's office, Peter and Guy, a woman, Melanie somebody, some AP's . You're taking a meeting with them tomorrow; they're really fast-tracking it. I'll call Robin, or do you want to?"

"Robin? Why? We don't need her at this stage—at least, I don't. I thought you and Kyle were going to work something out."

"We did, we'll give her a producing credit, she can do a lot of the shit work, the stuff you hate—dealing with Nelly's people, keeping all the suits happy, you know. Meanwhile you get me your wish list, the director, the talent, and I'll run them down, see who they'll let us use, who's available— can you get it to me by the end of the day?"

"It's already the end of the day, Sandro—"

"In the morning then, first thing. And be at Nelly's at six o'clock tomorrow, that's the only time they can do it."

"Oh, shit—how late do you think it will go?"

"Why? Don't tell me you already signed up to take care of the baby, *Bubbelah.*"

"As a matter of fact I have a very hot date with a very hot guy."

"Yeah? Well, tell him not to take the Viagra until midnight," he said. "You know how these meetings go."

CHAPTER
TEN

I went home, showered and changed and fed Tory, then drove back to Echo
Park in case the kids needed me. I was excess baggage, though—Jessie's
doula was there, a sweet-faced girl who radiated calmness, as well as the baby
nurse that Zach's mother had hired for a month. Nobody'd done anything
about the mess in the kitchen or the basket of dirty clothes on the first floor
landing, so I pretended I didn't see them either and followed the trail of
blankets, pillows, books, CDs, newspapers and gift boxes from Naissance
and Elegant Child up to the master bedroom. They were all sleeping—Rosie
was tucked in between her parents, all wrapped up like a *hamentaschen*. I
bent over them to inhale her sweet baby smell and her delicate little eyelids
fluttered open for a second or two before they closed again. When I planted
a soft kiss on her forehead, Jessie stirred and blinked hazily up at me. "Call
me later," I whispered, and backed quietly out of the bedroom. I turned at
the door and looked back at them, thinking 'thank you,' and something that
might have been a prayer, just in case anyone was listening.

After a quick fix of caffeine and chocolate, I got out the folder of notes
and emails that came in when the deal for the pilot was announced in the

trades. I put a few aside and opened my journal—actually it's a steno pad, one of the old fashioned kind with wire binding and lined pages. When I watch TV I jot down names of actors, writers, directors, and editors whose work stands out from the shit that fills so many prime time hours—the remakes of lame sitcoms with pretty, smart wives and fat, dumb husbands, the reality shows—it amazes me what people will do for their fifteen minutes, don't they have any dignity or common sense?—and the endless variations on *Law and Order*. I started doing it when I was running *Going It Alone*; I keep it up, if only to convince myself I'm not just wasting time when I'm watching TV, I'm working. I had the previous two year's worth of names on my computer, the ones before that on my Rolodex, a pre-tech relic like whiteout and carbon paper. Last Christmas Robin gave me one of those electronic organizers that does everything. "It's even got a tickle function," she told me, and for all I know, it's got one that pinches my ass, too; it's still in the box it came in.

I flipped through some dog-eared, coffee-stained cards and tried a few numbers, but I hadn't even gotten through the D's before I realized it was ancient history; people had left the business, moved up, down or out—their phones, which back then were all in one area code, had been disconnected, or the numbers assigned to a gas station in Burbank or a Domino's in Century City. A director who'd worked for me once was in the Motion Picture and Television Home in Woodland Hills, and thought I was his agent's secretary—a nurse took the receiver away from him and whispered that lately he was often in what she referred to as "another reality." Another one was in Forest Lawn. And a few who'd broken into features weren't interested: "But have your girl call my girl and set up a lunch so we can catch up on old times, "said one, and I agreed, knowing neither of us meant it. The pecking order is, film trumps TV, unless you're a movie actress over 40, which is when the small screen doesn't seem like quite so much of a comedown.

By the time I had a list of possible directors, writers, lead actors and supporting ones, it was nearly midnight. I hoped some of the same names would be on the network's approved list; talent with whom there were already deals in place, who had high Q scores or solid credits or the right look, who wouldn't make unreasonable demands or be difficult to work with. But I wasn't counting on it; I'd been out of the loop too long to know who most of those people were.

I crawled into bed, dog-tired but too keyed up to fall asleep. There was just too much stuff in my head, names and faces and memories. Like Dan, who played Lexy's boyfriend for a season—he was a sweet, funny, sexy Irishman whose drinking problem got too big to ignore, and the day I had to fire him he said, "Does that mean we can fuck now?" Since I didn't think it would be a mercy fuck—I'd been attracted to him since his first day on the set—we did. Then he got sober and stopped coming around; I heard he'd married a make-up girl and moved to Tarzana. And Deanne, a producer I spent a week with once at the Golden Door, developing a script that seemed like a good idea at the time but never got picked up. She was 40 then, desperate for a husband and a baby: "Not a husband who *is* a baby," she said as we lay next to each other on massage tables while skinny little Asian girls pummeled us, "which means nobody in the business." She'd quit soon after that and started a Jewish matchmaker business, something she dreamed up after she heard about a writer who couldn't get his scripts read because he didn't have an agent until he rounded up some buddies who were in the same fix, got some letterhead and a post office box in Beverly Hills and joined ATA: "Now he gets three mil a picture without even paying a commission," she told me at her baby shower; she married her second client, an orthodox accountant, and they live in Beverly Glen in a house that has two kitchens, one for meat and one for milk.

I remembered people I hadn't thought about in years until I saw their names in my files, especially the cast and crew of *Going It Alone*. After we won our first Emmy I'd taken the whole writing team and their families to Hawaii for a week—it was where I'd really gotten to know Livvy, a divorcee who had a laugh like a waterfall, red hair that corkscrewed out of her head, a promising career, two kids, a new boyfriend every other month, and a life that was a lot like mine. A few months after the trip she was diagnosed with ovarian cancer—when she died midway through our third season, having a successful TV show and making a lot of money and winning awards and being sucked up to stopped being like something I'd gotten away with and started being a job.

The hits just kept on coming but I absolutely had to get some sleep, so I gave up trying and swallowed an Ambien. Just before it kicked in, I remembered how Alex Carroll had looked at me; I slid my hand between my legs, but I was too tired for that, too. Besides, how many men say they'll call and never do?

He wasn't one of them—the phone woke me up at noon the next day.

"I've got a meeting that will probably go late," I told him. "It happened at the last minute, it's really, really important—"

"That important, huh?" he said, but his voice was light and teasing, so I explained about the pilot, the awful logistics of getting something made on such a tight schedule, how my life would be crazy busy until it was done.

He sounded genuinely disappointed. "Look, why don't you call me after your meeting, and I'll meet you somewhere—at least we could have a drink."

"It might be pretty late," I warned.

"It won't be too late," he said. "Whenever it is, it won't be too late."

Hope perfumes the air like lacquer in a beauty salon, and I wasn't immune; I didn't come out of Umberto's looking ten years younger, which takes more than can be done in a couple of hours and costs considerably more money, but I'd had my hair, nails and makeup done and I was wearing my lucky dress, a Diane von Furstenberg vintage wrap that was so old it was back in style again, just like me. I'd splurged on a pair of open-toed Christian Louboutin heels, and a new Pratesi briefcase, and I was as ready as I'd ever be.

First meetings on a new show are all smiles until the knives come out. Everyone jockeys for position, putting their favorites forward, figuring out who to suck up to and who not to bother about, who they want to work with and who they have to. By the time we broke up, we'd covered budgets and shooting schedules and locations, gotten together a wish list for Amelia and Clea and the key supporting roles, and agreed on a director—I didn't know him, but he'd done good work on a stylish FX series I'd seen a couple of seasons ago, and if he was available and we got on well together, we'd offer him the job.

One of the execs suggested a writer who'd done two of my favorite episodes for *Nip/Tuck*, and Robin mentioned someone from *Sex and the City* who had a movie script in turnaround but might be interested; she handed me a pile of scripts, saying "There are some good possibilities in here; I've made notes on them."

I'd had a quick conversation with Sandro just before the meeting started: "We're making her an assistant producer; we may have to give her a writing credit, too, we haven't worked that out, but meanwhile she'll do whatever you tell her," he said, "How bad can that be?"

I had plenty to keep her busy—put together an office, get phones and computers and copy machines and paper clips and people to use them, set up meetings with casting directors and location managers, and keep track of all the deadlines and schedules and details. Robin would be good at that—she was nothing if not efficient. I didn't have to trust her—and I didn't—but I'd be dumb not to use her, especially since I had to.

I left the meeting with a briefcase crammed full of tapes, scripts, casting books, names, phone numbers, and a to-do list that filled the fresh new steno pad I'd put in it that morning. It was nearly ten o'clock; I hoped Alex Carroll was still awake.

He was, and he was hungry, too, so we settled on Morton's, not the one where all the Oscar parties are but the one at the Meridien, where he was staying. The food was better, the room less see-and-be-seen, it was on my way home—sort of—and while the idea of going up to his room afterward crossed my mind, it didn't linger there. I remembered a conversation I'd had with Peggy once after we went to see Kathleen Turner play Martha in *Virginia Woolf*. We were mesmerized by the heat of her performance—she threw it off like sparks from a fire, and you could feel it even up in the second balcony, "I can't remember when I had that kind of passion," said Peggy at intermission. "Not for fighting *or* fucking. My libido has disappeared."

"I know what you mean," I told her. "Mine's like Al Gore's ambition for the White House—he may have put it away, but if there was any need for it, he'd know just where to look."

But as I drove down Wilshire, I wasn't thinking about having sex with Alex Carroll—not really. I was wondering if there was intelligence behind those gorgeous eyes, an expansive spirit as well as an easy laugh, if he was still curious, interested, interesting. If he was a grown-up, but had enough youthiness, too.

Most men who are the right age—which is to say, a few years north or south of sixty—don't. Rebecca, who's in my book club in New York, has fixed me up with several of them—widowers, usually, whose wives have recently died. ("Six weeks is too early, Sugar, but six months is way too late, you'll love him, he's a doll.") They seem old to me, stuffy and boring and just like their fathers, or mine, anyway, except they play tennis instead of golf and drive Benzes rather than Lincoln Continentals. It's as if the past never touched them, and the present doesn't, either. I went out with a man named Carl once, not even a widower, right after 9-11, who said he used to want to know how it all turned out—life, he meant—but he didn't, not anymore.

I did, though, so I touched up my lipstick, dabbed a bit of Preparation H under my eyes to shrink the bags, and brushed out my hair. After I gave the valet the keys, I sprayed a little *Vol de Nuit* in front of me and walked through it to meet Alex Carroll.

CHAPTER
ELEVEN

My opening line with a man is usually" Tell me about you." It's how Frances taught me to get a man interested. "Then it's off to the races, and all you have to do is nod in the right places and they think you're fascinating," she said, long before *Seventeen* gave me the same advice. Frances was years ahead of *The Rules*, and even *Cosmopolitan*; she said making a man think he's the world's greatest lover had the same effect, although how she knew that was a question she steadfastly refused to answer.

During my formative years, my mother delivered herself of many similar pronouncements about the opposite sex. I came to her once, confused and miserable, after I hit a home run in the last inning of the sixth grade softball tournament and David Carlson, who'd pitched it to me and on whom I had a desperate crush, walked another girl home after the game. ""Boys don't like girls who hit home runs—you have to learn to bunt," she told me: Like most of Frances' *dicta*, it was as depressingly true then as it is today.

I came to Frances not for comfort—she wasn't that kind of mother—but because she had a talent for men I would never possess; I've always known that. Effortlessly as breathing, she charmed them all—the butcher who gave her the best cuts of meat, the dry cleaner who pressed things at the last minute, the newspaper boy who went out of his way to place the *Star Ledger* on the Welcome mat at the front door instead of throwing it on the lawn. On Saturday night dances at the country club, all the men clamored to be her partner; at parties they lit her cigarettes and refilled her drinks, told her the latest gossip and jokes, while my father looked on proudly, as if it were all his doing.

Unlike the other married women in Short Hills, my mother had men friends—not lovers, at least not as far as I knew, just men who liked her company. One was the rabbi at the Reform temple whose wife, rumors had it, had had a breakdown and was at Bloomingdale's—the psychiatric hospital in White Plains, not the department store. Another was a slight man with a goatee who wore ascots and designed sets at the Paper Mill Playhouse. He and Frances were always re-doing one of the rooms in our house, and frequently they went off for the day to antique auctions in Pennsylvania or upstate New York. My father used to tease Frances about her *fagelah*, as he called him, but she said men like Donald were the only ones who really listened to women, because they actually liked them.

Uncle Max was the most interesting of Frances' men. He was distantly related to my father, a second or third cousin; he looked a little like Victor Mature, with those same bow-shaped lips and that wavy hair. In winter he wore a belted camelhair topcoat and a snap-brim fedora, and he drove a jaunty little dark green convertible. Uncle Max had been a captain in the Navy during the war, and later smuggled Jews from Cyprus to Palestine; according to Frances, he'd given the whole story of *Exodus* to Leon Uris, who never even mentioned him in the acknowledgments.

My mother liked having company. People had a good time when they visited, not just for cocktails or card games or dinner parties, but just dropping by, the way Uncle Max did, especially Sunday mornings. He'd bring white fish and lox from Katz's deli, and he and Frances argued over the crossword puzzle together while my father read the business and sports sections.

I used to spy on my mother and Uncle Max. It wasn't that I hoped to catch them in a compromising position, although that did occur to me after Mitzi Jacobson's father bought her a new Mustang because she skipped school to go see the Beatles at the Ed Sullivan Theater and encountered Mr. Jacobson coming out of the Algonquin Hotel with their next door neighbor. I just wanted to know how Frances did it, how she managed to make men fall in love with her.

Uncle Max was the first man I ever loved. When I was fourteen he committed suicide by intentionally driving his little sportscar at high speed into a stone wall. I mourned him not only deeply, but also dramatically—I threw myself on his grave at the funeral and had to be dragged away, wailing and carrying on and generally making a spectacle of myself. My parents sent me to a psychiatrist who told me I was suffering from a displaced Electra complex—the desire to replace my mother in my father's affection. Uncle Max was just a stand-in for him, reflecting an unconscious incest taboo. But that didn't make sense; since I grew out of diapers I'd known better than to compete with Frances for any man, especially my father, for whom no other woman but her ever existed.

I couldn't get Frances out of my head even after I got to the restaurant; as soon as the maitre d' led me to the table and I saw Alex Carroll again, disjointed bits and pieces of her advice flitted through my mind the way they haven't since the last time I met a guy and thought, *this could be him.*

He'd already ordered by the time I arrived—"The kitchen was closing and you said you hadn't eaten, so I just went ahead—steak is what they seem to do here, I hope you're not a vegetarian," he said.

"Not even close," I told him, "thank you, that was very thoughtful of you, I'm famished."

But it wasn't until we'd worked our way through the first bottle of wine that I realized I'd forgotten my opening line; I was suddenly conscious of the sound of my own voice, and realized I'd been talking nonstop since I sat down.

Even before the sommelier poured the wine, which had been waiting for my arrival, Alex asked all the questions. First he wanted to know how the baby was; I confessed I'd been too busy to check since she came home from the hospital: "A failure at my role already," I said, only half-seriously, "even unto the next generation."

"You'll have plenty of time to make up for it," he replied.

I was going to ask him if he had grandchildren—or, more diplomatically, children, since men are even more sensitive about their age than women are—but he short-circuited it by asking how my meeting went and what it was about. In order to explain, I had to give him a brief synopsis of how TV shows get pitched, sold, made, and what would or could happen to mine between now and when it aired. He asked good questions, not to flatter or impress me or because he had a great idea for a television series— which is what civilians always say when they hear you're in the business—but because he was really curious. He liked to know how things work.

"Enough about me," I said, "tell me about you." (*Finally*, I heard Frances say in my head).

His company had something to do with biotech data mining. "You've herd of the human genome project?" he asked, and I nodded. "Well, there's a ton of genetic data out there, some of which might—probably does—hold the clue to everything from curing cancer to creating a supernutritious tomato. Storing the data is relatively straightforward, but extracting or interpreting from it is extremely difficult. What everyone's looking for is a killer app to leverage the data into useful information."

"And you've got the killer app?"

"Not quite. What we've got is a data warehouse that's optimized for access of relationships....I'm losing you, aren't I?"

"Sort of," I admitted.

"It's too boring to go into unless you're a rocket scientist," he said. "That's who does all the heavy lifting, the rocket scientists. Quants, we call them. A lot of what I do is fly around the world trying to convince the really brilliant ones to come work for me. That, and poke around in labs and research centers where there's new data being generated. So we're attracting a lot of interest, especially from big pharmaceutical companies. I'm getting pressured by my board to at least listen to the offers. If the right one comes along, we'll probably take it."

"And then what? Would you retire?"

"Yes. No. I don't know," he said. "Maybe I'll do something entirely different."

"Raise llamas? Start a vineyard? Isn't that what you Seattle people do after you cash in?"

"Llamas are miserable creatures, they spit and bite, no thank you." He held up his glass to the light, admiring the deep purplish hue of its contents. "If I thought I could make wine as good as this I'd start a vineyard, but that would take too long."

"A lot of good things do."

His eyes changed then, ever so slightly—I might have missed the light dim in them if I wasn't looking, if I hadn't been noticing at that very moment how pleasing his features were, how nicely they fit together.

"Not all of them," he said. And then, more lightly, "After all, you didn't."

I laughed. "You mean I was too easy?"

"That remains to be seen," he said with a sweep of a nonexistent mustache and a leer that was meant to be comical.

I'd already given him the life and times of Sugar Kane, the abridged version, and he reciprocated—born in Pennsylvania, went to Penn State, tried a couple of different careers before starting his first company in Texas, "which failed spectacularly," he said. "Of course, that's the way everything happens in Texas," he added wryly.

"What a disaster that must have been," I said.

"No," he replied. "It was just a flop, like the one after that. A plane crashes into buildings and people die—that's a disaster." He signaled the wine steward for another bottle. "When you work for yourself, you win some and you lose some. But at least you get to do it your way, right?"

"Not usually. The meeting I just came from? Everyone there with the possible exception of the guy who delivered the Perrier has more of a say in how it gets done than I do. As was made glaringly clear, I'm hardly irreplaceable. There are plenty of people like me around."

"I doubt that," he said.

"You just haven't been looking." If you're good at flirting, you can say something that lightly, without feeling embarrassed; if you're not, but you're Frances' daughter, you say it anyway, hoping it doesn't sound stagy and ridiculous.

"Even if I had been, I could stop now," he replied, and then I *was* embarrassed. That's the kind of remark that I can never think of the right response to until the next day, after I've thought about all the things it could mean and dissected it with my girlfriends.

He didn't seem any more ready for dinner to end than I was. After we finished the wine we had brandy and coffee, and when the waiters began taking the cloths off the empty tables and giving us impatient looks, he walked me to the hotel entrance and waited while they brought around my car.

"I know you're going to be under the gun, but can we e-mail or talk on the phone until the show's done and I can see you again?" he asked, tipping the valet and taking the keys from him.

"I'd really like that," I said, and he smiled again. Then he stroked my cheek gently and kissed me lightly on the other one. Opening my car door, he handed me the keys and then he leaned through the window and kissed me again, on the lips this time. It wasn't a big production number, just a soft, promising kiss, but it was enough to send a "yes!" shooting down my spine like a bullet. When I drove away the heat spread all the way through me, and by the time I got home I was damp, exhilarated and exhausted, all at the same time.

The weeks before we began shooting in Vancouver went by in a blur of meetings, choices, decisions, frustrations and setbacks. Casting was the biggest problem. We still hadn't settled on the right Amelia; Candice was a regular at *Boston Legal* now and besides, the consensus was that we should go younger. That's what they always say about actresses. "Don't forget, high definition TV shows off every flaw in a woman's face," said our DP. "It shows off a man's, too," I replied, "and yet Kiefer Sutherland's a star. Go figure."

Looking for our lead actress was exhausting. I spent hours reviewing reels and auditioning women who were somewhere between *District Attorney* and *Driving Miss Daisy*, as Jane Fonda once put it, even after she had all that work done for Ted. There was a brief flurry of excitement when we thought we could get Cybill; despite her reputation for being difficult to work with and the inevitable comparisons that would be made between *Moonlighting* and *The Finders* (the show's working title, at least until they focus-grouped it), she had a big fan base, courtesy of two hit shows in television's decade of women, when brains were more than a fashion accessory and so was a sense of humor. With Cybill playing Amelia, we were all but guaranteed a network pick-up and commitment for a season, but if I let myself dwell on that I'd never get through making the pilot.

Cybill kept us hanging for a week before she backed out, but eventually we found our Amelia. Anne Tremont had had a promising film career, including an Oscar nomination for best supporting actress for an indie movie in which she played the mother of a dying child, but since then her career had stalled. She'd had a handful of "wife of" roles that were little more than walk-ons in forgettable blockbusters, but I'd seen her in a revival of a Mamet play in New York a couple of seasons ago and been struck by the supple intelligence and reined-in sensuality she brought to the role. I also liked her personally—she had a quick wit, a wonderfully dirty mouth, and warmth that seemed real rather than feigned.

That was one of my good days; a bad one, two days before rehearsals were due to start, was when Kyle's client, who'd been cast as Clea, announced that she was pregnant. She wouldn't be showing for the shoot, but if we got picked up we'd have to go right into fulltime production, and we couldn't shoot around her. You can get away with that in an existing series—although having Daphne obviously knocked up while she and Niles were courting wasn't *Frasier*'s best season—but not in a new one. The lawyers were worried about possible exposure to a discrimination suit if we didn't hire her anyway, since there'd been a verbal offer, but money took care of that, and we had a good alternative, an actress I'd wanted from the beginning. Chloe Padgett was the spunky younger sister in a family sitcom around ten years ago; she'd managed to avoid the usual fate of child stars, graduated with honors from Princeton, and made a couple of small, edgy films for which she'd received good notices. I was sure she was going to be fabulous, and so was Derek, our director.

That Chloe happened to be a friend of Robin's wasn't entirely a coincidence—Robin mentioned her while I was mentally casting the show before Nelly bought it. She wasn't a client of Kyle's, which probably pissed him off, but Robin was too ambitious to let boyfriend problems interfere with her commitment to the show.

Almost without my realizing it, Robin had become my second in command. People brought their problems to her—if she could solve them without involving me, she did, and if she couldn't manage to contain their clashing egos, she sought my assistance. I didn't give her the authority—she assumed it. But because it made my life so much easier I didn't rein her in, either. Preproduction is all details and the devil lurks in every one; they weren't my strong suit, but Robin was so organized I left a lot of them to her. We were cordial, even friendly; on the surface, at least, our relationship hadn't changed. I still didn't trust her, not the way I had, and with no one else to do it for me I had to watch my own back; the more indispensable she became, the easier it would be for her to fuck me over again.

In addition to Robin, I had good producing partners; still, mistakes were made, as politicians (used to) grudgingly admit. Some were mine, some were other people's, but ultimately I'd live or die by them—or, as Alex said in one of our conversations, "You mean live *with* them. You don't die because a deal or a project goes south, there's always another one, you learn, you get smarter."

"Or you don't," I said—it had not been one of my better days.

"Aah, Sugar, you'll bounce. From what you tell me, you always have."

We'd gotten to know each other surprisingly well in that quasi-intimate way e-mail makes possible. And we'd fallen into the telephone habit almost immediately. One night he called while waiting out a weather delay at the airport in Pittsburgh. "I drove through my home town today," he said. "Stopped in a bar I used to drag my old man out of. The same guy still owns it. I walked in and he said, hey, Alex, how're they hanging, like it was just a few days since my last time in."

"How long ago was that?"

"The day I graduated from high school," he replied. "Nothing's changed. They've still got my old football jersey hanging from the light fixture. Guys I went to school with—they're still there, too. Punching out of the mill and tanking up before they go home and take out their frustrations on their wives."

When he told me the first time we talked that he'd grown up in Pennsylvania, I didn't picture a steel town near Pittsburgh. I thought he came from some genteel, Gentile exurb on the Main Line, where he'd been raised in a sprawling house with green lawns and dogs, maybe even horses. Everything about him, his manner and his manners spoke of that kind of confident, privileged upbringing.

"Not by a long shot," he said. "My old man and my brothers worked in the steel mill like almost everybody else in town. I always knew that wasn't for me, and I was a pretty decent quarterback so football was my way out. I got a scholarship to Penn State and then I signed with the Oilers."

"You played professional football? Get out!"

"For three years, until my knee went out. Then I got a job with a medical products company in Houston. I majored in biology in college and always had an interest in science, so it seemed like a good fit. I wasn't crazy about selling, but I liked working with doctors and scientists, understanding what they needed and figuring out what I could do to solve their problems. So when I got a chance to move into product management at a bigger company in the same field, I took it."

"And then?"

"I met a couple of very smart researchers from UT who had a promising device that could potentially revolutionize the process of identifying genetic markers, so I raised a little capital and went into business. We had eight people on staff and our office was a garage in Austin." He laughed shortly. "We were sheep to be slaughtered—we had no idea how to run a company. I was commuting to Houston every weekend I could get away, which wasn't all that often." He was quiet for a minute. Then he said, "That was the first flop. And some time between that one and the one after that the marriage fell apart, too."

I knew his ex wife had custody of the dog—she'd also gotten the kids, two boys who were 8 and 13 when they split up. "That must have been hard on them," I said.

"We had a pretty good relationship until the divorce. After that, they were like strangers. Didn't want to see me, didn't want to talk to me…I don't know what she told them, but it did the trick. I guess they thought they had to choose between us. Chris was always very close to his mom, plus he had that teenage boy thing going, and poor Evan, he was mostly confused. It was obvious they didn't want to spend time with me so I didn't push it."

"You mean you never saw them?" I couldn't imagine what that would be like. Even when Ted and I couldn't manage to be civil to each other, right after we split up, we made sure the kids weren't dragged into our *mishegas* and that they had the closest thing possible to equal time with both of us.

"A month in the summer, sometimes a week at Christmas. We did guy things together so we didn't have to talk very much—skiing, camping, diving. But the older they got the more they missed their friends and routines and the less a part of their life I was."

"Where are they now?"

"Chris was in Saudi with Aramco, now he's in Houston with Halliburton. And Evan's an astrophysicist at Palomar. Chris got married a year ago—I haven't met his wife, just got an announcement. I think he took the divorce the hardest. Evan and I e-mail back and forth pretty often, but it's been a couple of years since I've seen him."

I heard the echo of sadness in his voice. Although I vowed I wouldn't be one of those women like some of Frances' friends in Florida who sit around the bridge table and complain that they never hear from their kids unless they're broke or in trouble, I get antsy if I don't touch base with mine on a regular basis. I don't need to know every detail of their lives, just enough to assure me that they're okay. Lately I'd been talking to Jessie a couple of times a day—after all, who else but a grandmother is interested in the texture and color of a baby's BM's? And although Paul wasn't as communicative as his sister, he stayed in touch, too; in fact, he'd called the day before, ostensibly just to say hello, but really because he was worried about me.

"Are you sure you're not working too hard?" he asked.

"Of course I am," I told him. "You know what it's like—you lived through *Going It Alone*."

"Yeah, except for that episode where the kid catches his mother in bed with a guy he's never met," he reminded me. "I barely survived that one." He'd taken a lot of teasing from his friends because of the show, which was not, I told him a hundred times, about us—which of course, it was. "But seriously, Ma, you shouldn't overdo it. After all, you're not as young as you were then."

"Of course I'm not. Out here they count your age in dog years, but relatively speaking I'm in pretty good shape for a 400-year old broad. Why? Do you know something I don't?"

I don't believe in all that woo woo stuff, but sometimes I wonder whether the umbilical cord that attached Paul to me for nine months still exists, somewhere in a parallel universe, binding us together now the way it did then. His "thing" reassures me—if there were something really wrong with me, I believe he'd know it. And if he did, he wouldn't let my insistence that there was nothing deter him.

"Nope. Just checking," he said.

"I'm fine, darling, really I am. Don't worry about me. Now tell me about that girl you were seeing—Kelly, is it? Is it serious?"

"Don't be one of those mothers," he groaned. "If and when it is, I'll let you know. You're sure you're okay, huh?"

"I'm sure," I said. "Besides, you'd know if I wasn't."

I'd told Alex about Paul's "thing" in one of our e-mails, and it fascinated him. "Did you ever have him tested?" he wrote back.

"No—Ted wanted to, but you know how kids are, he didn't want to be different. He says it's not something he can control—it comes and goes, and it's only about us, not other people. His best friend in high school had leukemia, and he never had a clue until Josh went into the hospital," I typed.

"If he ever changes his mind, let me know. My former brother-in-law is a psychologist at Baylor. He's been doing research along those lines."

The next time we talked, I mentioned the brother-in-law. "You're still friendly?" I asked.

"Sort of," he replied. "We have dinner together a couple of times a year when I'm in Houston."

"Is that where you met your wife?"

"No, we grew up in the same town."

"Oh?" Now we were getting to the good stuff. I could have cared less about her brother; I wanted to know about her.

"Did she want out of there, too?"

"Not quite the way I did. Her father didn't work in the steel mill—he owned it. As you can imagine, he wasn't exactly thrilled when she brought me home."

It was like one of those star-crossed young lovers movies from the fifties— *Splendor in the Grass* meets *A Summer Place*. I was already casting it in my mind.

"Were you crazy about each other?"

"Well, we were crazy, anyway. We got married on the field at half time during my first Oilers game. She called her folks an hour before and told them to watch."

I could hear the ice cubes tinkling in the glass. "I wanted her," he said. "She was this fantasy of mine, the blonde princess in the castle on the hill—no kidding, it was this huge Tudor thing, a real castle. So I took her away and bought my own castle—actually, it was a split level—and put the princess in it."

"Except you didn't live happily ever after," I said softly.

"No, we didn't. Except I didn't get that till I came home one night and my key wouldn't work in the front door."

"Quite a way to find out," I murmured.

"I'll say. I had no idea. We hadn't been fighting or anything—in fact, that morning before I left we'd even made—I'm sorry. That was probably in the category of too much information. Or too much scotch. Or you're too good a listener. Or all of the above."

You can be the best listener in the world, but if a man doesn't want to talk it doesn't matter. That night, though, Alex was in a ruminative mood, and I was all ears. "I was a lousy husband," he said after a while. "I don't mean I, you know, fooled around or anything. I was so involved in what I was doing, what I was trying to do, I just didn't notice how unhappy she was."

I wondered what he would have done if he had, but I didn't ask. I'd told him that night at Morton's that I'd been divorced for a long time, to which he'd, responded "My good luck, his bad." It hadn't sounded like a line, not the way he said it, and it felt sincere and spontaneous. Or maybe I just wanted to think so...of course, I believed Bill Clinton when he said he didn't have sex with that woman, too.

All that personal stuff came in bits and pieces over the weeks before we started shooting. E-mail is a truly wonderful thing, and so are cell phones with no roaming charges. He called me once from Paris, where he was trying to lure some rocket scientist to come to work for him, and another time from Sydney, where he skipped out early during a symposium on the human genome project and went scuba diving on the barrier reef, which I gathered was the Mount Everest for divers. "God, Sugar, you'd love it. One of these days we'll have to get you underwater. It's a whole different world down there."

"It's just like L.A. only the sharks don't have law degrees," I said. "The idea of breathing through a tube while Jaws circles around me terrifies me."

"We won't go anywhere there are sharks, I promise," he countered, and that was all he said about that. If 'one of these days' ever rolled around—if things progressed to the point where we actually went somewhere together—I'd prefer Paris or Barcelona—I look better in a little black dress than a bathing suit.

Very quickly, it seemed, Alex Carroll had become a familiar presence in the landscape of my mind. Often I caught myself wondering where he was, what he was doing. I looked forward to his phone calls and checked my email more than usual in case he'd written. Once three days went by without hearing from him. "Do you think this means it's over?" I asked Carrie.

"How can it be, it hasn't started yet?" she said. "Just kidding, Sugar, you'll hear from him, I know you will. Relax."

The next best thing to talking to Alex was talking to the girls about him. They didn't tell me not to get carried away or caution me that he probably had some fatal flaw—on the contrary, they were almost as pleased as I was. "Sugar Carroll—it has a nice ring to it," said Carrie. "Are you doodling it in your notebook yet?"

"Not quite, but close," I told her. "Fortunately, I've got a show to get on the air."

"Rich and single," said Suzanne. "Don't let him get away."

"Don't do that thing you do," warned Peggy. "You know, the if-he-likes-me-this-much-there's-probably-something- wrong-with-him thing."

But when he asked me to stop over in Seattle on my way to Vancouver, I hesitated.

Preproduction was almost complete; rehearsals were going well, and although we'd make small changes in the shooting script up to and including the first day of principal photography, we'd be ready to start in less than a week. Alex broached the subject of coming to visit him in an email, which gave me time to think about it—and of course, to canvas the girls.

"You don't have to analyze it to death," said Carrie. "You meet a guy, he seems nice, you get to know each other, he's just what he seems to be, and he likes you."

"Or he isn't, or he doesn't."

"So? You've survived worse in the man department."

"Let me count the ways," I sighed. "Seriously, though—"

"That's the problem. You're taking it too seriously. Go now, worry later. Have a good time. Get laid, for God's sake!"

Suzanne said the same thing, but more frankly. "Listen, Sugar, these days you really are more likely to get blown up by a terrorist than find a guy. And before they fly a plane into your bedroom, you better get your ass in gear. He sounds nice. Rich, too, which doesn't hurt, believe me." Suzanne married poorly but divorced well. Her first husband—she never remarried, but she always refers to Greg as her first husband—was a TV news anchor who's been paying her a third of his salary since forever, the price she exacted when he threw her over for a pretty blue-eyed blonde reporter who looked remarkably like Suzanne did two children, twenty-five years and that many pounds ago. Matthew, with whom she's lived for several years, is a poet, painter and raconteur who tends bar at Odeon to keep himself in Zegna shirts and hand-tooled boots; As Suzanne says, unlike Greg he's always in a good mood, is nice to people even if they can't advance his career, and most important, he thinks she hangs the moon.

Peggy, as usual, hit the mark closer than Carrie or Suzanne. "What are you afraid of?" she asked. "That something good might happen? That he might turn out to be the One? And that he might walk out with your stuff?"

We're all captives of our own romantic history, and mine is one of struggling between the urge to merge, to lose myself in a man, and the equally powerful yen for independence. If there's a middle ground, not the quicksand of intimacy that can disappear you or the hard-packed earth where your footsteps leave no trace, I haven't found it yet.

"You know me, I'm just a simple bitch wid' a bad attitude," I said.

Peggy sighed. "Well, leave it home and go. If he turns out to be a jerk, so what?"

"What if he doesn't?"

"You'll think of something else to worry about."

CHAPTER
THIRTEEN

I hadn't told Alex exactly when I was arriving, only that I'd be checking into the *W* late in the afternoon, so I was surprised to see a limo driver holding up a sign with my name outside of baggage claim. "Mr. Carroll sends his regards, Ma'am," he told me. "He said he'd see you at six."

When I got to the hotel, the concierge handed me a note saying the same thing. A bellhop took my luggage and led me upstairs to my room, where a gorgeous flower arrangement, a basket of fruit and cheese, and a bottle of Chateau Ste. Michelle chardonnay awaited me. A nice beginning, I thought; maybe this wasn't such a crazy idea after all.

It was a mild day and the sun was shining, so I put on my walking shoes and set out to explore. I'd been in Seattle once before, when Jessie was looking at colleges, but I hadn't seen much of the city, so I headed down to the waterfront and strolled past the old wooden piers that jutted out into the bay. In front of the aquarium a little boy jumped up and down with excitement—"Me going to the fishie zoo!" he told every passer-by as his mother struggled to collapse his stroller. I passed clam bars and souvenir shops, ferry terminals and restaurants, a dock where Sikhs in wrapped turbans leaned against their cabs smoking while they waited for passengers to disembark from the Victoria hydrofoil. The day was warm for early April; in the park the trees had greened up, the azaleas were blooming, and tight little buds had formed on the roses. Two teenage boys were playing Frisbee in a graveled crescent between two parallel walkways, one for wheeled traffic and the other for pedestrians. Elderly couples strolled arm in arm, skaters and bikers whizzed past on a sinuous trail, and the air was fragrant with salt-tinged breezes and freshly blossoming trees.

I made my way down to a small beach where dogs chased sticks and balls into the water and a couple of teenage girls blithely ignoring the surgeon general's warnings held their aluminum-shaded faces up to the sun. Taking a seat on a peeling log deposited on the beach by a long-ago storm, I lit a cigarette and thought about all the things that could possibly screw up the shoot or go wrong in postproduction, thus sinking our chances of getting a series out of the pilot, even a commitment for a short season.

My anxieties inevitably terminate in a worst-case scenario, which tends to calm them by reminding me that even a fuck-up of unimaginable humungousness that meant I never got a job in the business again wasn't a death sentence. I'd survive—I wouldn't starve, the people who love me still would, and screw the others, and I'd still have my health, family, and sense of humor.

Well, my sense of humor anyway. I wasn't so sure about my health. As a matter of fact, I'd been feeling shitty for most of the last week. It wasn't anything specific, just a transient tightness in my chest or occasional dizziness when I stood up after I'd been sitting in one place for a while. I hadn't been sleeping well, and I had new aches and creaks in places I hadn't, before.

That's the thing about getting older—you don't know if what you're feeling is just because you *are*, or it's symptomatic of something else. *Like a heart condition.*

Let's not go there. Not now. Let's think about something pleasant, like Alex Carroll. And then my heart quickened—it really did, the same fluttery feeling you get when you're pregnant and the baby moves for the first time, just a little higher up and to the left. Only I didn't need a doctor to tell me I was fine.

On the way back to the hotel I passed an elegant looking lingerie store; on an impulse I went inside. According to show biz legend, the great impresario Flo Ziegfeld insisted that all the showgirls in his follies wear silk beneath their lavish costumes. "But Mr. Z., why throw away money on something the audience doesn't even see?" asked his accountant. "Ah, but the ladies *feel* it, and *that's* what the audience sees," he replied.

When I came out of the shop my wallet was a lot lighter and so was my mood. I hadn't bought new underwear for a man in a long time—not since Jan.

When I met Jan I was in a particularly *zaftig* phase—not just overstuffed in places, which I've always been, but spilling dreaded back fat out of my 36C wonder bra and excess flesh over the waist of my size 10 jeans. Ten certainly isn't skinny—in Los Angeles it's considered obese—but after Paul was born I said goodbye to single digit sizes in everything but shoes. That was the beginning of my shoe jones, because even when nothing else fits, they do.

But Jan loved my fleshiness. The day after the night we first slept together we went to a Modigliani exhibit at the Met, and he drew me into an adjacent gallery featuring the pendulous, full-bodied sculptures of Gaston Lachaise. "I like these better than those," he said as we stood in front of a series of drawings, studies for the large bronze that dominated the room. "They're his wife, Isabel. I think they're beautiful."

"Really?" I'm always interested in who and what men find beautiful—personally, I think it all has to do with their mothers, but since I'd never met Jan's I could only speculate.

"Picasso said, you give a man looking at a picture everything he needs—breasts, hips, legs—and he'll put everything where it belongs with his own eyes. He'll make the kind of body he wants."

"And you'd make...her?" We gazed at the huge bronze sculpture, and he ran his hands lightly down my body, as if tracing its outline. Then he turned me around so my back was to the other couple in the gallery, putting one hand on my breast and cupping my sex with the other. Through the thin fabric of my skirt his thumb found one cleft and his middle finger a different one. An "Oh!" of surprise escaped my lips; my thighs loosened and my knees went weak. I would have fallen if he hadn't cupped my crotch more firmly and pulled me against him. "I'd make you," he murmured into my ear.

Alex Carroll probably preferred Modigliani, but there was nothing I could do about that so I took a long, hot bath, liberally softened with Bliss lemon and sage-scented oil thoughtfully provided by the hotel, and slathered Body Butter all over me. Then I took the tags off my new purchases and slipped on the filmy, lace-trimmed La Perlas before inspecting myself in the full-length mirror on the closet door. At a certain point in life, you don't undress for romance, you drape for it, concealing your flaws and hoping for the best. I didn't know if Alex Carroll would be watching when I disrobed that night, but just in case, I was ready.

I saw him in the lobby before he spotted me. He looked even better than I remembered, in a three-button black cashmere blazer over a charcoal striped collarless shirt and gray flannel slacks. A smile lit up his face as I approached—he held out his arms and I stepped easily into them, close enough to accept a friendly kiss on the cheek before I leaned back to look at him; damn, those eyes were something else.

"Hey there, Sugar," he said. His faint drawl stretched out the words— his voice, familiar from our phone conversations, was deep and melodious. "I'm really glad you decided to come."

"So am I," I smiled back.

The valet was waiting with his car, a dark blue Saab convertible with the top down.

"Do you mind?" he asked as I settled myself in the passenger seat. "I'll put it up if you'd prefer."

"No, please don't. I love convertibles. My first car was an MG, I was hooked."

"The TD?" he asked. "I had one of those, too. A dark green one."

"Mine was blue," I said.

"What happened to it?"

"I traded it in for a station wagon."

He grinned. "So did I."

We drove down a steep hill and turned south into a neighborhood of cobblestone streets and turn of the century streetlamps atop intricate wrought-iron standards. "We've got about twenty minutes before the sun sets," he told me. "I thought we'd have a drink on my deck—it has a wonderful view—and then go across the street for dinner."

We were in Pioneer Square, he explained. "The settlers used to skid the logs down from the top of that steep hill to the saw mill at the bottom. That's where the expression, skid row, comes from." He slowed to allow a horse-drawn carriage to clop past us. "A new factoid for your collection." In one of our conversations I'd told him that my favorite book was *Brewer's Dictionary of Phrase and Fable.* "Here's a little present for you," he said. "I picked it up over there at the Elliott Bay. It's a great bookstore." I tore off the kraft paper wrapping and picked out a brightly colored, oversized paperback. *Americanisms: The Illustrated Book of Words Made in the U.S.A.*

"A man who listens when a woman talks—what a concept!" I said. "Thank you so much—I love it."

A few minutes later he pulled up in front of a red brick building similar to the others in the neighborhood, He clicked the remote, the garage door opened, and he drove in and parked. The garage elevator creaked its way to the top floor, where it opened directly into a brick-walled loft with wide planked floors and towering ceilings. Late afternoon light poured down from the top of an open staircase in the center hall: "The view's upstairs," he said. "I sleep down here but I live up there."

The upstairs took my breath away. From floor to ceiling windows facing north and west, the city and Sound were spread out before me. Beyond an elevated viaduct, the jagged peaks of the Olympics framed a bay busy with water traffic. At one end of it, tall orange cranes, like side chairs for giants, lifted ocean-going containers off the decks of a freighter. At the other, a passenger liner strung with gaily-colored flags tooted its horn in preparation for departure. Between them toy-like boats with billowing sails swerved and jibed: "A little early in the season, except for the really dedicated sailors. There are a couple of those on my team who've been putting in a lot of overtime lately, so I told them to take the afternoon off and enjoy the weather."

"You must be a popular boss," I said.

"It's no big deal—there aren't that many nice sunny days in Seattle this time of year. Why don't you go out on the deck? I'll fix us drinks and bring them out."

The hum of viaduct traffic was muted somewhat by the deckscaping. There were bamboo trees in terra cotta pots set among wooden planters that were thick with bushy grasses and ivy hung from the railings. A squat stone Buddha regarded me serenely from a ferny corner between two slatted wood benches. To the north the city skyline twinkled with lights from tall office buildings; the silhouette of the Space Needle, backlit by the setting sun, was like a spindly tinker toy off in the distance.

Alex brought us each a glass of wine and we stood in companionable silence, watching the last sliver of sun sink behind the mountains, splashing the sky with streaks of purple, red and orange. A wind came up and I shivered; my blazer was silk, but beneath it my blouse was thin and sheer, and my trousers were a light gabardine.

"You're cold," he said. "We'll go in."

"Not quite yet." The sky seemed to hold its breath until the sun's reflections faded and the last streak of color disappeared. "Now," I said. "Now we can go in."

I looked around. I could imagine Alex here, working at the crescent shaped rosewood desk, reading in the Eames chair with his long legs stretched out on the ottoman, or watching the flat screen TV on a wall opposite the windows from the brass-studded leather couch. From almost anywhere in the room he could watch the ship traffic in the bay, the sunset reflected in the towers of glass and steel at the water's edge or snow-capped Olympics.

The shelves surrounding the TV held artifacts as well as books that tended toward history, biography and science. There were some African masks, a cluster of framed photographs, a football trophy and a cowboy hat. Terry Gross's familiar voice issued from Bang and Olaffson speakers on one of the shelves; he pressed a button, silencing it.

A compact but functional-looking kitchen, all black glass and stainless steel, was divided from the living room by a granite-topped counter where Alex had set out a dish of olives. It was definitely a man's room, but there were some whimsical touches, too, like a pair of steel bar stools with their backs bent into profiles of two jut-jawed faces, and a Peter Max triptych that reminded me of a Grateful Dead poster. But what made me laugh out loud was the coffee table. Its base was a Dalmatian, lying on its back with its pink Nike-shod paws holding up a glass rectangle. I bent down to examine it more closely: its eyelashes were made of curly black telephone cord, and its pink satin tongue flopped contentedly out of its mouth. The lettering on the small sign sewn to its belly said *The Bitch in the House*. I looked up at Alex, who smiled and said, "Doesn't every house need one?"

When we left the loft we walked across the street, through a wrought iron gate into a narrow courtyard surrounded by brick buildings. We went into one of them to a ground-floor restaurant and were greeted by a dapper man in his sixties with a rose boutonnière in the lapel of his suit.

"Good evening, Mr. Carroll," he said.

"Hi, Carmine, nice to see you. This is my friend, Ms. Kane."

"Good evening, Ms. Kane. Welcome to Il Terrazo. Your table will be ready in a few moments—meanwhile, may I offer you an aperitif in the bar?"

The barman looked up as we came in. "Campari and soda?" he asked, and after a look at me for approval, Alex nodded. We took our seats at the bar and I looked around. It was busy but not crowded with well-dressed people sitting near us or at the leather banquettes against the wall. Relaxed, end of the day laughter and the quiet hum of conversation surrounded us. "What is it they call their neighborhood pubs in England?" asked Alex. "Their locals? Well, this is my local. It also happens to be one of the best restaurants in town."

"Convenient, I'd say. Does Carmine deliver?"

"Only for very good customers," he said. "He's owned this place for years. You can't tell it's here from the First Avenue side of the building—you have to know what you're looking for."

"And you do."

"Usually," he replied. "But sometimes I don't know what that is till I find it."

The salmon was so fresh it must have swum up from the waterfront and climbed onto the stove and the rest of the meal was equally good. I kept Alex laughing through dinner with stories about La La land and a few about myself. He was a good audience until Frances got inside my head again— "Men say they want a woman with a sense of humor, but that only means they want you to laugh at *their* jokes"—and I stopped talking.

"Your turn," I told him. "What's the project you've been working so hard on?"

"It's so complicated I don't totally understand it myself," he said. "We're looking at a new way to combine data from molecular genetics, treatment protocols, that sort of thing. They cure diseases in labs all over the world hundreds of times a day, but unless they know why, they can't do it a second time. That's where data mining comes in. We collect a lot of information, but we don't always know how to use it."

"Like the government. The FBI still hasn't sifted everything they knew about 9-ll even before the attacks. Or about terrorist activities since then."

"Like that," he agreed.

The waiter proffered a dessert tray, but I shook my head. "I think we'll take a check, Giorgio," said Alex, and then, to me, "How about I walk you back to the hotel? It's only eight or nine blocks from here—are you up for it?"

I felt a pang of disappointment. So I wasn't going to explore the lower floor of the loft—not tonight, anyway. "Sure," I agreed. "Why not?"

He took my hand as we crossed the street, and held it all the way back to the *W.* Ignoring my aching toes, I managed to keep up with his long stride until he realized it; he slowed down, and we made our way out of the Square, past antique shops and taverns and coffee bars and bookshops, onto a walking path between the waterfront and the viaduct. Eventually we turned east, onto a broad avenue lined with office buildings, stores, and a striking modern building that zig-zagged up a steep hill in glass-encased boxes that seemed to float in air. "The new library," he explained. "It's by Rem Koolhaas. People either love it or hate it."

I loved it—if it had been open I'd have insisted on going in. "Tomorrow," he said. "I'm in meetings most of the morning, but my driver will pick you up and take you around until I meet you for lunch."

"That's not really necessary," I protested. "I can find my way around. I don't want to be a bother."

"You're not, and you probably can. But he'll take you to the airport in time to make your plane." As we approached the hotel, his Blackberry beeped—he stopped, read the text on its screen and frowned. "I'm sorry I can't deliver you to your door," he said. "I have to get back to the office—something's come up, a glitch I've got to deal with. Do you mind?"

"Of course not," I replied, a little disappointed—I was still hoping to end the evening in a more romantic manner.

As it turned out, I did. In front of the hotel he pulled me into his arms for a long, satisfying kiss—a real one this time, not a buss on the cheek. I inhaled the faint fragrance of Issey for Men, one of my favorite scents, and his arms tightened around me. "I'm really looking forward to getting to know you better—a whole lot better," he said when we came up for air.

"So am I."

"You can't stay over till Sunday?"

"No—I ought to be up there now, the crew's been shooting background for a couple of days already. Besides, you're going to Hong Kong tomorrow night."

"I could put it off."

"But I couldn't."

"Can't blame a guy for asking."

"Ask me again."

"Count on it," he said, and in spite of all the men who've said things like that over the years and forgotten them the next day or week or month, I believed him.

CHAPTER
FOURTEEN

If you happen to be having a heart attack, Seattle is the best place to do it. Five minutes after the clerk at the Elliott Bay called 911, the EMT's had me in their ambulance with an oxygen mask over my face and a pressure cuff on my arm. My cell phone kept ringing until one of the guys took it out of my jacket pocket. "Hello? Never mind who this is, who are you?" He bent over me. "Do you have a son named Paul?" I tried to nod but the motion made my head hurt even worse than my chest.

I'd checked out of the hotel around eleven, leaving my bags with the concierge, and was killing time at that bookstore near Alex's apartment until I met him for lunch. I picked up enough paperbacks to get through the next three weeks—mystery novels are better than sleeping pills, and even though eventually they rot your brain, you're not hung over in the morning. I was on the last stair down to the basement café when I suddenly felt so lightheaded I had to grab the railing to steady myself. My chest hurt and I couldn't breathe, so I decided not to. The next thing I knew, I was flat on my back, and a woman whose long hair tickled my nose was exhaling hot little whiffs of *eau de vanilla latte* in my mouth. When she started thumping on my chest as if she was trying to push it into the floor, counting "one one hundred, two one hundred," I muttered, "Stop that!" even though it hurt even more to talk. She lifted herself off me and raised a triumphant fist in the air, Rocky-style—people around her clapped their hands, and then someone threw a coat over me, and someone else bent down and told me not to worry, help was on the way.

I could give you all the medical details, but stuff like that is very boring unless it's about you. Suffice it to say that the punch line to what turned out to be a very unfunny bit of cosmic comedy was that while I'd had every symptom of a heart attack, I hadn't actually had one. What I'd had was a return visit from the octopus, except that this time it really *was* an octopus.

"*Takotsubo*," said the doctor two days later, when my heart was pumping again and they'd gotten my blood pressure back up. "From *tako*, meaning octopus, and *tsubo*, which means bottle. See this?" He held up an X-ray of my heart and pointed to a funny shape on one side, sort of like a vase with a round bottom and a narrow neck. "It's Japanese—it's a trap they use to catch octopus. What happens is the muscle cells of the heart go into paralysis—here, close to the aorta. Only the upper part of the heart contracts, which means it can't pump out enough to give you the oxygen you need. It's not very common, except in elderly Japanese women. I don't think we've ever seen it in someone like you."

Someone not Japanese or someone not elderly? Although it was an interesting factoid, medically and etymologically—I knew a writer on *House* who'd be fascinated—I didn't really care. I was just glad to get a straight answer from somebody, especially this Dr. Kaplan, who had a much nicer bedside manner than O' Neill. I was relieved that he was not only Jewish (okay, I'm stereotyping here, but forgive me, I just had an attack of the killer calamari) but the head of cardiology, too. "What happens in *takotsubo* is that the left ventricle goes into akinesis—that's a temporary paralysis—and balloons into this shape," said Kaplan. "It looked like an MI—you had all the signs. So we did an emergency cardiac catheterization. Your coronary arteries looked pretty good—not great, but okay, and you should talk to your regular cardiologist about that—but the ventriculogram was the tip-off. Lucky the attending recognized it."

I wasn't clear about when it first hit me that I might be dying. It must have been in the ambulance; if I am, I remember thinking, someone ought to know. And then the reassurance that of course Paul would calmed me down like Valium. Or maybe it *was* Valium.

He'd caught a plane as soon as he talked to the ambulance guys, and when I came to some time that night and saw him, he looked different. Not like the Paul I picture when I think about him—then he's a kid, not even twenty, a college dropout who hasn't figured out who he is yet. But there in the room, half-asleep with his head slumped over his chest in a chair next to my bed——that couldn't be a bald spot on his crown, could it?—he looked like a man.

They kept me stoned enough for the next 24 hours that by the time I was fully conscious it was of how bizarre my circumstances were—being a patient in a strange hospital in an unfamiliar city, called Charlotte by people who don't know that's not who I am even if it *is* my name—and how relieved I was not to be there alone.

"So what you're saying is that she didn't really have a heart attack, it was something else?" Paul asked the doctor.

"It wasn't a myocardial infarct, which is what people usually mean by that. Unlike most MI's, it's completely reversible and doesn't leave any permanent damage, although technically, it's still cardiomyopathy," he replied.

"I had a kind of heart thing a few months ago, in New York," I began when Paul interrupted me with a muttered "Dammit, I knew it!" but I ignored him. "Could this be related to that?"

"That's hard to say. I got your hospital records from your insurance company and talked to a Dr. O'Neill this morning. He thought *takotsubo* was a very interesting diagnosis."

"Meaning, he should have thought of it?"

"It's easy to mistake for the real thing," he said diplomatically. I could imagine what my ex-husband, the King of Torts, would do with *that* in front of a jury if he knew—which he wasn't going to. "Paul, you didn't call your father, did you?" I asked.

"Of course not, why would I do that?" he said. "I called Jessie—Ma, don't look at me like that, she's your daughter, she has a right to know."

"But you told her I was okay, right? That it was just a mistake, I'm fine, I'll call her when I get to Vancouver?"

He and Kaplan exchanged one of those looks that men use instead of words when they're patronizing us. "Maybe before then," said Paul.

While it helped to have a name for what was wrong with me, just like in TV or analysis, what's really important is what happens next. "How do you get the octopus out of the bottle and the bottle out of my heart?" I asked the doctor. "And when can I get out of here?"

He frowned. "While this is a temporary condition, your heart is still in a state of dysfunction. We have to normalize the ventricular wall motion—in effect, treat the paralysis—before you go anywhere. We've got you on medication to increase your blood pressure, but you're still not getting enough oxygen. You're going to need to be monitored carefully for a while."

"What's a while?"

"Anywhere from a week to a month, depending," he said.

"What?" I was horrified. "I can't stay here that long!"

"You're doing exceptionally well. There's been a marked improvement in the last 24 hours."

"So it might be less than a week?" If I had to, I could spin some kind of story to account for a couple of days.

"That's very doubtful. You need to be treated in a hospital."

"Well, for a few days, maybe. But then can't you just send me home with whatever drugs I need? I thought hospitals couldn't wait to get you out the door these days. I'll take it very easy; I'll get plenty of rest, I promise," I said while Paul snorted in disbelief.

By now the cast and the rest of the crew were already in Vancouver. I'd told Robin I was stopping in Seattle on the way up there to see this incredible man I'd been getting to know; how can any woman not tell something like that to her girlfriends? (Of course she wasn't one, not any more, but that's beside the point—or maybe it *was* the point.) So she might just think I was deep in the throes of lust and had taken an extra couple of days off. But she'd never believe I'd be unprofessional enough to blow off the whole first week of a shoot of my own pilot for any man, not even George Clooney. If I told her the real reason, I was fucked. Word would get around fast—she'd make sure of it. And even though I hadn't had a real heart attack, just something that looked like one, it would be over. Not the show—they wouldn't postpone the pilot, and even though I like to think I'm indispensable, the truth is I'm not. With a script, a director, and a couple of other writers to make the changes that always get made when the cameras finally get rolling, they wouldn't have any problem replacing me. Besides, they had Robin.

Both Paul and the doctor thought my suggestion about going AWOL from the hospital was crazy and it was clear that they weren't taking it seriously. I was trapped here, with a sleeping octopus stuck inside me, until he decided to go away and take his bottle with him.

"This thing I have, what caused it?" I asked.

"Have you been under a lot of stress lately?"

"No more than usual," I replied. "Why?"

"Stress precipitates *takotsubo*. When the brain releases an overload of stress hormones, the blast paralyzes the muscle cells. The Japanese call it broken heart syndrome."

"I don't have a broken heart." *Au contraire*, I might have said, thinking for the first time since they carried me out of the bookstore about Alex—I wondered what he thought when I didn't show up or call.

"It's not only grief that causes it—other kinds of emotional trauma have been known to bring it on, too. If your heart doesn't give out before the initial burst of hormones subsides—and you were lucky you got to the hospital as fast as you did—most people recover."

"Can it happen again?"

"Possibly. It comes back in less than 20 percent of cases, but as long as you take care of yourself and avoid stressful situations you should be okay."

Paul turned to me after the doctor left. "Why don't you just level with the studio, tell them what's going on?"

"Because if I do, I'll not only not get another shot, I'll never eat lunch in Hollywood again. I'll just be an old lady with no career and some kind of heart trouble that sounds like sushi."

"You could do other things. You could finish that novel you're always talking about."

"I tried and I couldn't. Listen, baby, your mother *needs* this job. She needs another series. It's not about the last chance at the gold ring; it's about the gold. The money. I need it."

"*Going it Alone*'s still in syndication, isn't it?"

"Not really, nobody picked it up this year, that's over."

"But you've still got the house."

"And the mortgage that goes with it. If this show doesn't make it, I don't, either. I'll have to sell the house, liquidate what's left of my stocks, and live on that until I can collect social security. Which even then—especially then—will never provide a standard of anything I'd call living."

"You could ask Frances for help," he said.

"What? And have her tell me it's still not too late to go to law school?" I said, and we both laughed.

Paul was just a kid the last time I had to ask Frances for money. I'd had a long dry spell, financially speaking, after the book tanked and before the show took off. During that year and a half my roof fell in, my transmission fell out, my tenants disappeared owing four months of back rent, and I needed three root canals plus porcelain crowns to cover them. I also had no work—the free-lance market had less tread than the tires on my six-year-old station wagon.

All their married life, Frances got an allowance from my father. Often they argued about what it should cover—the drycleaner, the gardener, the paper boy, the maid when she stayed to help with their dinner parties or the new dress she bought for the Bar Association dinner. It wasn't heated or angry, just a kind of low-level bickering that was the *lingua franca* of my childhood. I never heard him tell her they couldn't afford something, just that money didn't grow on trees. "He used to say if I knew how much money he had, I'd spend it," she told me after he died and she learned how much it was—not a fortune, but substantial enough, she said, "so I never have to go into one of those awful places, I could have nurses around the clock, right in my own house, as long as I live. And Esme, of course."

Even when my father was alive—when, technically speaking, it was his money—my mother always told him what to do with it. Which was usually to give it to us if we needed it but only after we agreed that we were helpless without her, the way you have to do in 12 step programs before you can get better.

That was how she was about money—then, anyway. My brother would never ask, but my sister Joan was a genius at getting Frances to open the purse strings. Of course, she really was helpless; she was in and out of funny farms from Menninger's to McLean for twenty years, and during her manic periods she went on crazy spending binges. But for me, asking Frances for money was a last painful resort, an admission of guilt for having been so foolish as to think I could get along without her, so shortsighted as not to have taken her advice and chosen a more stable career or gotten a better divorce settlement. I didn't do it unless my back was to the wall, it was years since I'd had to, and I wasn't going to do it now.

"So it's the money thing you're worried about, right?" asked my son.

"It's that, and the show, too—I'm really proud of it, I wanted—want—to see it made. To see it through. To be doing what I know how to do again, knowing a lot more now than I did then. To feel like I'm somebody."

He took my hand and squeezed it. "I always thought you were somebody. I knew you were. You still are."

I felt a rush of love for my son so strong it overwhelmed me, made the breath catch in my throat and the tears well up in my eyes.

"And so are you, darling...so are you. You are a wonderful man."

It's hard to keep your life from happening to your kids, especially when you're a single parent. If you're busted or flush, depressed or delirious, having sex or not having it—whatever's going on, they know it. All you can do is try to keep your own shit from affecting them—the stuff you know about, not what you don't figure out until years later, after it's too late. But once they leave home, your problems are your own business, and they're too busy figuring out their own lives to think about you, including Paul, unless he senses something physically amiss, the way he does with that odd gift he has. So it was strange to be talking to him the way I would to a grown-up. Not just any grownup, but a friend I trusted, someone who loved me and wouldn't leave me to deal with the octopus alone. Someone who was strong enough so that if I had to lean on him, I could.

It took me a while to figure out how to handle my other immediate problem. Paul had gotten himself a room in a B&B near the hospital, and I sent him to retrieve my luggage from the concierge at the *W* and bring me some things I needed, including my computer and briefcase.

"Ma, you heard what the doctor said. The primary cause of *takotsoba* is stress. In fact, that's the only cause. I don't think the computer is such a good idea," he said.

"The doctor didn't say I couldn't."

"His exact words were read, watch TV, whatever you feel up to."

"I won't know what that is unless I do it. At least bring my briefcase. I can't just ignore my responsibilities. I have to look at the schedule so I can tell Robin what to do."

"They won't let you use your cell in here."

"I know, but I can call from here—I'll use the room phone. I'm going to tell Robin where I am."

He looked relieved until I added, "I'm just not going to tell her why."

CHAPTER
FIFTEEN

"Your appendix?"

Robin was surprised, but she believed me. There was no reason not to—it could happen. In fact, it recently had, to the governor of New York, and I made my story as close to the newspaper accounts of his as I remembered. He'd spent a couple of weeks in the hospital after his appendectomy, a good cover in case Kaplan decided to hold me longer than a few days. None of the stories had made any fuss about how old he was; a hot appendix is an equal-opportunity excuse, even though I'd had mine out when I was 15.

I ran down my last-minute list with Robin, who'd already taken care of the niggling details I hadn't quite wrapped up before leaving L.A. Everyone had arrived, she said; she'd scheduled a meeting the next morning with Derek, the director, and Luca, the unit production manager. "I want to be conferenced in on that," I told her, while Paul rolled his eyes in disbelief. "And you'd better bring Sharon in, too." She was the other writer I'd brought on after the script was approved and could make any necessary changes. But Robin would be the go-between between Derek and Sharon and the actors, who actually have to say the words and frequently have strong feelings about what they should be. Sometimes their suggestions or objections are good, other times they're useless or obstructive or both, but it's the show runner or producer's job to keep everyone happy. Robin would be good at that, probably better than I am, I mused: as I knew from my own experience, she was very good at shining people on.

Producing a show is walking a line between being in control and interfering. A good producer doesn't interfere unless it's absolutely necessary to get the show done on schedule and on budget. I'd hired good, experienced people and I needed to let them do their jobs. What Robin herself lacked in experience, she made up for in intelligence; she was thorough and prepared, and, most important, people liked her.

It doesn't matter if you're making widgets or movies; people like to do business with people they like. What casts and crews hate are producers who create havoc on a set by second-guessing everyone and being assholes just to assert their authority. The good ones don't have to; they know how to guide, lead and support their people, and when to get out of their way and shut up.

The fact is, I was lucky as hell to have Robin. This time I really needed her. I just didn't know what it would cost me.

I got frowned at a lot that first week. The nurses complained that I was screwing up their schedule when I was too busy on the phone, soothing, cajoling, putting little fires out, to accommodate their demands that I have another MRI, get my IV changed, give them more blood or X-rays or urine. Kaplan showed up one morning just as FedEx arrived with the tapes of the previous day's shooting, and shook his head. "Did I tell you that stress caused your condition? Did I tell you that it comes back sometimes, and the next time, it could kill you?"

"This isn't stressful, it's just watching television," I said as I popped the tape into the VCR. "Really, I'm fine. Aren't I? Isn't the octopus going away?"

"You're making very good progress," he replied. "But if you get right back into the situation that caused the stress in the first place, it won't matter."

Paul said pretty much the same thing and so did Jessie, when she flew up for the day to see me. I was thrilled that she'd brought Rosie; I put her in my lap on her back, tickling and kissing and making sounds and faces that elicited her infectious, throaty little giggle, which made me and Jessie laugh, too.

"Really, Mom, it makes no sense at all for you to go to Vancouver," she said. "You've just had a major heart attack—"

"I did *not* have a heart attack!" I said indignantly.

"Well, you *could*, that's what the doctor said."

"I could also trip and break my neck or get hit by a car, but that's not a reason to stop walking or driving," I said.

She was exasperated. "Then how about this? How about Rosie? Isn't she enough to keep you from trying to kill yourself?" She picked the baby up and opened her blouse to nurse her.

"I'm not trying to kill myself. And she's the light of my life, but if I don't have a life—if I can't work—so what? That's a big burden to put on a little thing—to be the reason someone gets up in the morning."

There were times right after the divorce when my kids were practically the only reason I did. If I hadn't had them—if they hadn't needed me—I'd have stayed in bed, I was so depressed and miserable. Ted betrayed me; even if I could get past it he didn't want to. It's easy to say it was only my pride that was hurt, but that's not true. My confidence in my own judgment was destroyed; in spite of the occasional other women, I'd believed he loved me and our life together until he told me he didn't. I felt rejected sexually as well as abandoned, worried about having to fend for myself in the marketplace again, fifteen years older and even less convinced of my desirability than I was when Ted settled the issue by marrying me. Except as it turned out, he hadn't. I wasn't. And because of my inexplicable need to prove that I didn't need him either, I was also in dire financial straits.

So I got out of bed and got on with my life. I had no choice. I had responsibilities. Which, if they're in good hands, grandchildren aren't.

"Please don't worry, Jessie. I'm not pushing myself. I'm here, aren't I?"

Tears filled her eyes. "I couldn't bear it if you weren't," she said.

I reached for her, across the baby between us. Her thin arms encircled my neck. "Don't you let anything happen to you. Don't you dare," she sobbed. "I still need you."

Paul came in one afternoon while I was giving Robin a carefully staged update on my condition—"No, it's not serious, nothing like that, just a slower than expected recovery, just between you and me they're not letting me out until I move my bowels, and the food is so awful here that I—that's right, probably before the weekend or maybe right after—I know everything's going well, I talked to Derek, he had a question and couldn't reach you...I know, you were taking care of Anne, yes, well, we'll just have to get her a makeup person she likes, we're not relighting the whole scene because—Of course, that was more important, Robin, you're doing a fabulous job...no, you really are. It's like you've been doing it as long as I have. I really lucked out, having you on board. And you know I'll make it good, money and credit-wise, don't you? That's right...we trust each other. We'll work it out....okay. 'Bye."

According to Robin, so far things were going so smoothly that few people had noticed my absence. Derek was a good director; we'd spent enough time together to know we wanted the same thing from the actors, and he was getting it from them. The AD's seemed to be making good use of all the extras we'd hired, the sets looked good, especially Amelia's office, and the castle the location scout found in the mountains not far from our Vancouver soundstage would do nicely.

I was pleased with the cast. My leads were good—Chloe as Clea was a fascinating combination of child and adult, insecure and independent at the same time, touchy and difficult but brilliant and quick-witted on the job. Anne wasn't quite as I'd imagined Amelia—a little less steely, a little more maternal—but in the director's hands it worked; I could see how Clea needed that from Amelia, how it might even have made her confident enough to take the kind of risks the script calls for with such élan.

Watching other people make a movie of something you wrote can be like getting knocked up by an alien—there are little things about whatever's born of the union you recognize as having come from you, but the others... well, who the hell knows? But what I was seeing wasn't only pretty faithful to my original concept and script, it was better. Even without me.

"You're not going to quit before the show is done, are you?" Paul had given up trying to talk me out of it; he just wanted to be sure I'd be "sensible," as he put it.

"You don't have to be on the set every day, you know," he said.

"No, I don't," I agreed. "But I do have to put in an appearance now and again. Talk to people in person. Tell the cast I like what they're doing. Head off any problems."

"How often?" he wanted to know.

"Couple of times a week. But I should be in the production office more often. Mornings—I could just do a couple of hours, then not come back after lunch. I'll go back to the hotel and concentrate on not feeling stressed. Go to the gym. Meditate. Let go of my ego, as you JewBus say."

"Ma, if you let go of yours you'd have separation anxiety," he said dryly.

Paul was the only one of us who took religion seriously. He'd lived in a kibbutz for a year before he went to college, and traveled in India after he dropped out, when ski season was over. He went back to Dharmsala a couple of years ago for six months and when he came back he brought a spiritual practice I didn't totally comprehend but that seemed good for him—at least it didn't make him do something bizarre like wear an orange robe and beg for money at airports, like his high school buddy Scott Greene, who I recognized at LAX once when I was catching a flight somewhere. Nor had Paul grown *payes* and joined the *Lubavicher*, either. He studies Tibetan, he goes to a local zendo, and he's happy. "Your father used to meditate to lower his blood pressure," Frances said. "He didn't shave his head, did he?"

"I just want you to take care of yourself, that's all," said Paul.

"And you'll know if I'm not...I'm only kidding, Paul, I intend to." I hugged him. "Have I told you that I'm glad you were here?"

"Did you think I wouldn't be?"

"Of course not. I always knew you'd be here for me. I just didn't really, you know, *know* it the way I do now."

"Yeah, the octopus opened your eyes."

Maybe it had. Not just to the fact that my kids were grown-ups now, but that I could count on them in a crisis. Count on them to care. And with that comforting thought, I hugged and kissed my son and told him to go have dinner or see a movie, I'd be fine.

CHAPTER
SIXTEEN

I told everyone the same story I'd told Robin and swore my kids to secrecy, too. "If it hadn't been for Paul's thing, you wouldn't have told us, either," Jessie said. "Honestly, Mom, I don't know what the big deal is. Okay, I get why you don't want people in the industry to know, they won't let you finish the show or ever work again, yada yada yadda. I don't like it and neither does Zach, or Paul, for that matter, we think it's totally fucked but it's your decision. But not tell your family? Your friends? What's *that* about?"

"I just don't want them worrying about me."

"But they love you!" she said, exasperated.

"I know they do. And that's why I'm not telling them."

I could hear her sigh over the phone. "Have it your way. But I've told that lie about your appendix to Frances and Uncle Peter and Aunt Joan and so many other people that my nose looks like Barbra Streisand's."

And so had I. Carrie, Peggy, Suzanne, Hallie—they thought I was in Vancouver shooting the pilot, and there was no reason to tell them otherwise, even though it was lonely in the hospital and sometimes I wished I could talk to them about what had happened. But like everyone else, they had problems of their own, and I didn't want to be one of them. The one person I hadn't figured out how or what to tell was Alex Carroll.

I'd stood him up for lunch, and by the time I realized I was going to live I knew I couldn't tell him why. I finally sent him an e-mail in the middle of the week, apologizing—there'd been an emergency on the set, I'd had to leave in a hurry, I'd had a wonderful time and hoped to see him again when my life wasn't so crazy, etcetera. But I wasn't ready to lie to him in person yet.

I didn't want him to think about me the way I was thinking about myself—like I was frighteningly, immediately, mortally vulnerable. As if I were going to die, not in the comfortably far off future but at any minute.

In fact, I probably wasn't. By the end of the week, Kaplan was looking positively upbeat and said he was taking me off the medication they were giving me intravenously.

"Does that mean I can leave?"

'Not yet," he said. "When you were brought in, your heart was only able to pump out around fifteen percent of the blood it contained. Now it's up to nearly 40."

"What's normal?"

"Fifty to sixty percent. I won't discharge you until it's been at least 50 for three days. I'd be happier with a week."

"I can't stay that long."

He shrugged. "That's up to you. But I think you're making a mistake."

The next day there was a knock on my door. "Ms. Kane? I'm Marian Nelson. Dr. Kaplan thought you might be interested in some reading material."

She handed me a stack of pamphlets. The one on top was titled "Stressed For Success?" and the others were variations on the same theme.

"These have some exercises and techniques that can help you manage your condition," she said. "I'd be glad to go over them with you."

"Maybe tomorrow," I said. "I'm a little tired now."

Paul didn't leave Seattle until I did—he insisted on accompanying me to Vancouver in the town car the studio sent to pick me up. I was glad for the company, despite his uneasiness about my decision to go back to work so soon. Before he left me at the hotel, he reminded me that very few people remarked on their deathbed that they wished they'd spent more time at the office. "I know you have to finish this job," he said. "Just don't let it finish you, okay?"

"It will take a lot more than that to finish me," I said. "Go. Don't worry. I'll be fine."

I was on the set at six the next morning and hardly anyone seemed to notice it was the first time I'd made an appearance. I hung back, not exactly hiding, just watching and listening. We were only half a page off our schedule, which was pretty good considering, and so far the results looked fine. Derek was happy with the performances he was getting from the cast, especially Chloe – "She's going to be huge," he said, "You'd better sign her to a run of the series contract while you can."

"If there *is* a series," I said. "First things first."

He'd replaced the actor who played Clea's boyfriend, who'd turned up too loaded to work for two days in a row. "Vancouver's a good place to be if you have a habit," Robin told me, "You can walk through Gastown and get what you need in a heartbeat." And he and Robin were still mulling over whether to replace Denise Gale, who'd auditioned so well for the role of Amelia's assistant but was a disaster on camera.

"She might work better as a voice, off screen," Robin suggested. "You know, someone we never see. She has that neurotic New York thing going, that voice is like a cross between Rhoda Morgenstern and the Nanny."

"No wonder I hate her," I replied. "I'll tell the DP to cover the shots so we can do it in post if we want to."

"Actually, I already mentioned it to Jim," she said. "He's taking care of it."

A lot of what a show-runner does is wheedling, cajoling, pacifying and ass kissing, and Robin outshone me in all those departments. When it came to dealing with guys, she deployed her southern charm like a weapon, honeying them this and sweetieing them that so they ended up convinced that all her good ideas were actually theirs—sort of the way she'd operated with me, too, except I always knew when she was shining me on. It was a big temptation to let her continue to run the show, but if I didn't want my baby to get completely away from me, I had to let people know who was really in charge. When a man does that, he's being assertive—when it's a woman, she gets labeled ball-buster, bitch, or worse. So I took a cue from Robin and did my own version of honey this and sweetie that, oh you big smart man, however did you think of that, only without the southern accent. I used to do that feminine soothing and stroking and accommodating not only well but automatically, although the older I get, the harder it is—or, as Suzanne says, "Welcome to the Fuck You Fifties."

It's also exhausting, and at night I fell into bed too tired to worry that I might not wake up the next morning—a recurring fear the whole time I was in the hospital. On the suggestion of that woman Kaplan sent into my hospital room with the pamphlets I hired a yoga trainer who came to my room every morning: Exhaling my breath the way she demonstrated was like bathing my heart in champagne and I visualized little bubbles spreading oxygen through my bloodstream. At night they brought dinner in while we all went over the next day's schedules and call sheets and reviewed the dailies, Back at the hotel I swam laps in the hotel pool or had a massage before I went to bed. Meanwhile we kept on shooting, and by the time Nelly came up with her entourage from L.A., we were less than a week from completion and looking pretty good, all things considered.

Then disaster struck. Gerard, who played Jean Paul, the semi-retired jewel thief, collapsed on the set and died on the way to the hospital. It was a massive stroke; nothing could have saved him. His part wasn't finished yet—he had one key scene left and two smaller ones, and it was way too late to replace him with another actor. I sweated through thirty six straight hours with my production and writing staffs, re-jiggering everything to cover Gerard's absence, trying to ignore the clammy, woozy light-headedness that came and went, wondering if every twinge in my chest was the octopus and taking my pulse when I thought no one was looking. All the while I kept telling myself, *Sugar you can do this, you can handle this, this isn't really endangering your health, it's just for a little while, when we wrap you'll go to bed for a week.* Or, as Frances always said, *you can sleep when you're dead.*

Gerard's death hit us all hard. He was a favorite with everyone from his co-stars to the lowliest member of the crew; he was one of those people who make coming to work a pleasure. Plus he'd been perfect for his role, exactly what I wanted when I created it. He and Anne had such good chemistry together I'd been thinking about bringing him back as a continuing love interest for Amelia if the pilot made it to a series.

Calling Gerard's wife in Paris to break the news, saying those irrevocable words to a stranger, a disembodied voice on the phone, was heartbreaking. Both Derek and Robin had offered to do it, but it was my responsibility, although they came with me to the airport to meet her plane.

When Gerard's shockingly young widow arrived to claim his body she was accompanied by his first wife, a woman close to my own age. She handled the formalities of his death as briskly and efficiently as a Parisian concierge, insisting on making the arrangements for the repatriation of his body and presenting the necessary papers for Danielle's signature, and it was she rather than Danielle who came to the set and thanked Gerard's colleagues for their condolences. It was almost as if Gerard had two widows—Julia, who'd shared thirty five years of his life, managed his career and raised his children, and the younger, prettier version, Danielle, for whom he'd publicly humiliated and abandoned her. But she was tender with her successor, and Danielle was equally respectful of her; "It's so European, isn't it?" said Robin.

"When Mitterand died, his wife and his mistress both came to the funeral, along with their kids," I replied. "After all, it was the French who invented the *fait accompli*."

Finally, it was done. We wrapped two days over schedule with a minimum amount of complaining from the higher-ups, who didn't have much choice; even I couldn't be held responsible for an act of God. Besides, they thought they could capitalize on the tragedy: Gerard was a popular actor who'd broken into films after a long career as an entertainer, a sort of Johnny Holliday type, and the pilot would be his first as well as his last TV performance. "We own the rights for that revival he did of the Maurice Chevalier role in *Gigi* a few years ago," Nelly told me. "If we air it before the pilot, we might get some extra press out of it. Of course, that all depends."

On whether you screw it up in the post, she was probably thinking, but I tried not to obsess about that. I had five days before post-production started, and I was going to spend three of them with Alex Carroll.

CHAPTER
SEVENTEEN

Except for a brief fling once with a stuntman, I've never gone in for guys who took risks the way Alex did. He routinely ventured into places anyone with a brain in their head would never voluntarily go—under oceans, up cliffs, to the summits of mountains, and, more immediately, twenty thousand feet up in the air. I could feel the beads of sweat clam up on my forehead.

"Would it help if I had a uniform with epaulets and a shiny badge?" Alex teased as he helped me into the cockpit and motioned me to a seat next to his.

"It would help more if we took a ferry there," I grumbled. "Is this your plane? How long have you been flying?"

"About ten years," he said, doing something with the controls. "This is the second plane I've owned."

"What happened to the first one?"

"I traded it in—why, you think I crashed it?" He smiled. "Ferries take forever. I have a cabin in the San Juans, and the schedules are spotty, especially off-season. It's quicker to fly. And more fun."

"Is that where we're going?" I asked, and he nodded.

"Unless you have any objections," he said. "It's quiet, pretty low-key, but I think you'll like it. And I'm not a bad cook. Okay?"

"It sounds wonderful," I said, trying to sound like I meant it. Which I did, except for how we were getting there. I'd left the arrangements for the weekend up to Alex; I'd made enough decisions for a while. "I'm ready to be the girl for a change, let someone else be in charge," I told Carrie on the phone that morning as I packed my things, carefully folding the La Perla underwear I'd bought for my last date with Alex.

"Ri-i-ight," she said knowingly. "Because you're so good at that."

When Alex called from downstairs to tell me he'd arrived, Robin had just knocked on my door to say goodbye, and we took the elevator downstairs together. "You didn't tell me he was *so* Clint Eastwood!" she whispered as he came toward us. He was wearing black jeans, Tony Lama boots and a leather jacket, and he looked like a kazillion dollars. "And those eyes," she added, "Wow! Have a fabulous time, Sugar –you really deserve it."

There was nothing wrong with what she said, but it sounded just the other side of patronizing. Or maybe I was overreacting—- *Get over it, Sugar,* I told myself as we left the hotel, *concentrate on him, not her.* Which is just what I was doing as I buckled myself into the co-pilot's seat and Alex went through his preflight checklist. "Stop looking so worried," he said. "She's just had her annual maintenance check-up."

"What about you? Have you just had yours?"

His eyes changed color then, although maybe it was just the reflection of the sun streaming through the Plexiglas window in the cockpit. "I have a flight physical every year," he said tightly. "Chances are good to excellent that I won't keel over 'till we're on solid ground."

I wish I could say the same thing, I thought, but once we leveled off I opened my eyes. We were flying over the straits of Juan de Fuca between Canada and Washington; it was a beautiful day and there was barely a cloud in the sky. "Look—down there," said Alex, and I followed his pointing finger to what looked like enormous black logs gliding along on top of the water. When he flew lower I saw they were actually whales; as we circled above them they breached the surface and fell back in the water again and again, emitting bushy clouds of vapor through their blowholes, slapping the sea with their tails and spraying huge gouts of water in every direction. "Spy hopping," said Alex, "That's what they're doing, it's a new word to add to your list. They're migrating up from Baja this time of year. If the weather holds, we can kayak with them tomorrow."

"Isn't that dangerous?"

He grinned. "Isn't everything that's worth doing?" Then he saw the look I gave him. "It's actually very safe. I've taken my 83 year old mother sea kayaking, and she loved it."

"So the risk gene is inherited, huh?"

"My mother's idea of risk is making left turns or playing the quarters slots in Atlantic City."

"Making left turns?"

"Mmm hmm. If she can't get where she's going driving straight or turning right, she doesn't go. Even if there's a left turn arrow on the signal and it's green. Okay, now—close your eyes again, we're landing."

Actually, I thought, it would be fantastic to be out on the water among those graceful giants instead of watching from a distance. "Thank you so much, that was an amazing experience," I said as he turned off the ignition.

"The flight or the whales?"

"Both." It was true—once I got over my initial nervousness, being in the cockpit with him was okay—all right, better than that. Some women get an erotic charge from men who know how to do stuff, whether it's fly a plane or put on a roof. It's why guys in tool belts stir us up—the sheer masculine physicality of it. (It's also why when I remodeled the studio, it took me twice as long as it should have and cost twice as much as it was supposed to—I had an affair with the contractor, and even though the place looked terrific, when the job was over I was miserable and lonely.)

We got into a beat-up old Volvo parked at the little airport on the island and drove almost to the other end of it before we came to his house, a weathered log A-frame set amid towering evergreens on a bluff facing the Sound. Inside it was simplicity itself—a great room whose salient feature was a river rock hearth with a fireplace big enough to stand up in, furnished in Early Summer Rental with an oval rag rug in front of the hearth, a faded velour La-Z-Boy and oak rocking chair flanking it, and a long cracked leather couch with rump-sprung cushions.

"The accommodations are up here," he said, leading the way upstairs. "Take your pick," he said. "Garden or ocean view?"

It was obvious which bedroom was his, so I pointed to the other, which overlooked the back of the thickly forested property. I'd wondered about the sleeping arrangements, rehearsing several potential scenarios the way I always do, but Alex took the awkwardness out of the situation. "Good choice," he said, "that's the one with the hot tub. Do you want the ten cent tour first, or would you rather unpack?"

There wasn't much more to see. The house looked like the kind of place that's been in someone's family for years, which according to Alex it had been. "I saw it right before the kids put it on the market," he said. "They were sad to think whoever bought it would probably tear it down because there were a lot of happy memories in it, and I told them I wouldn't, I didn't want to change anything, which clinched the deal. There was already an outdoor shower on the deck off the guest room—I just added the tub."

Outside the air was a potpourri of fragrance—grapey-smelling wild irises, the salty tang of the sea, and the breeze-borne aroma of pine and fir trees. At the top of the wooden stairs that led down to the beach, Alex picked up a galvanized tin pail. "The tide's out," he said. "Do you like oysters?"

We picked them off the beach until we'd filled the bucket and then he rowed us out to a buoy a couple of hundred feet from shore. Pulling a crab pot out of the water, he beamed and tossed it in the boat. "These are the first ones I've pulled in a month," he said. "Looks like dinner's on mother nature tonight. She must really want to impress you."

"So far she's doing a very good job," I said. "And so are you."

By the time we got back to the house we were thirsty, so we drank a bottle of white burgundy while he put the coals on and cleaned the crab and I made a salad and set the picnic table on the front deck. We drank half of another one while we grilled and ate the oysters, and the rest while making a slurping, licking, happily messy meal of the crab. By the time we finished I was a little bit tipsy, and maybe he was, too—it was hard to tell, I didn't know him well enough yet.

"How about a little Risk?" he said after dinner.

"Wasn't that the plane trip?"

"Not hardly," he said. "I mean the game. There's a Monopoly set here too, but somehow I think you're more the take over the world type. Or we could watch a movie. Or maybe you're tired and want to turn in."

"Risk is a great idea," I said. "I haven't played for years."

We set up the board, making ridiculous boasts and pooh-poohing each other's moves. "This'll wipe you off the map," I said at one point; "You and whose army?" he snapped back, which sent us both into gales of laughter. Maybe you had to be there but trust me; it was more silly fun than I'd had in years, especially without being stoned.

In between moves we talked about how much the world had changed in our lifetimes. "Everything seems a lot more fragile now, doesn't it?" I said, telling him about the man who said he didn't want to know how things turned out any longer, they could only get worse. "Have you ever felt that way?" I asked.

He thought about that while he pondered his next move. "Maybe," he said. "But not now."

"What changed?"

"I met you," he said simply, and then proceeded to march his army into Russia.

"That was Hitler's mistake, too," I said, moving my own forces closer to the Chinese border.

"Ah yes, but look—that makes you vulnerable over here, and here, too."

I was thinking about what he'd said just before that move into Russia, and in a few decisive thrusts he won the game. "My mother says you should never outshine men at anything—they don't like it," I said, and told him about the sixth grade softball game. "You're saying you let me win?" he asked, amused.

"Do I look like that kind of girl?" I teased.

"I don't know yet. But I didn't come to lose."

After a couple more games, I was yawning. "I think I'm ready for that hot tub," I said.

"Want company?" he asked easily.

"Not right away. Maybe after."

"Enjoy. I'll be down here."

I soaked in the tub for a while—it was starlit and peaceful there, the only noise the wind sloughing through the trees. Then I rinsed off in the outdoor shower and slipped on a knee-length green silk nightshirt I'd purchased in the hotel boutique in the Four Seasons. Standing at the top of the stairs, I watched him for a couple of minutes—he was sprawled out on the couch, a book open on his chest, his eyes closed. But then he opened them, and looked up at me.

"Everything okay?" he said. "Do you need anything?"

"Yes," I said simply. "As a matter of fact, I do."

One of the things I've noticed about getting older is that often the anticipation of getting your ambitions realized or your fantasies fulfilled is better than the payoff. Or maybe it was always that way. But having sex with someone isn't like winning an Emmy or seeing the sun set over the Nile with Omar Shariff (back in the day, that is). It comes with its own set of anxieties, especially when you're not, well, young anymore. Forget the vague worries in the back of your mind about whether your heart can stand it—obsess over your usual issues with your naked body, which is not what it once was; as

Nora Ephron says, anything you didn't like about your body at 35 you'll be nostalgic for at 45. Or as Frances put it after my father died, "If I ever sleep with a man again, it would be good if he were blind."

Fortunately, Alex had his hands full of silk before he slipped the nightshirt over my head and we got into bed, and by then he was naked, too.

I had forgotten how it felt to be in a man's arms, skin to skin. He was a slow, tender lover—too much so, I thought at first, after more foreplay even than Jan, who always liked the first couple of acts more than the climax. I hoped Alex wasn't having trouble getting it up and avoiding the issue; once they're past the stallion stage, a lot of men do. You always have to tell them it's not their fault, you're fine, it doesn't matter, when you don't mean anything of the kind—it is, you're not, and it does. Toward the end of our affair, Jan had trouble that way—once a man has embarrassed himself sexually with a woman, usually he doesn't want to risk it again.

But soft and slow wasn't Alex's problem, just his style. He took my hands in his, kissing my fingertips one at a time and sending delicious little shivers of anticipation up my spine. Then he lifted each breast, tonguing the nipples erect until they pulsated with an insistent rhythm—*more, more, more.* Nothing existed except my need to have him inside me, and when he finally entered me it was slowly, deliberately, and only part way. Then just as deliberately he pulled back and out, lifting himself away so the tip of his cock was just out of my reach. The only part of him that touched me was his tongue, which curled itself around mine and probed the tender membrane underneath, gently at first and then demandingly. We breathed each other's air until it was hot and steamy inside the cavern we made of our mouths; mine was an entire erogenous zone with all feeling and sensation centered there until the first small, sweet release that rippled through me. Groaning in desperation I pulled him back inside me, coming a second later and then again and again.

He was the kind of lover who takes as much satisfaction in a woman's pleasure as his own. I don't remember how many times he brought me to climax before he gave in to his, but later, as I drifted off to sleep, I thought, *Sugar, this time you've not only been well and truly fucked, you **are***.

I was sure of it when he brought me coffee and croissants in bed the next morning. I couldn't help channeling Jane Austen—*Reader, I married him*—even while I reminded myself as I always did that if it looks too good to be true, it probably isn't.

But if Alex Carroll had a fatal flaw, it wasn't evident that weekend. Saturday we went kayaking, which I really enjoyed; the sea was calm, and although we didn't encounter any whales, we saw a baby dolphin with its mother and a couple of bald eagles flying overhead. I got on a bike for the first time in years, one of the old fashioned ones with fat tires and no gears, and we rode into town—"It's only a few miles," Alex said, "and it's flat, we're on an island."

"So was Krakatoa," I replied, but he was right, it wasn't hard, although I knew if I didn't swallow an Advil when we got back to the cabin I'd be sore the next day. *You'll be sore anyway,* said my left brain to my right, *after all that unaccustomed fucking.*

In the general store a woman with well-muscled arms and graying hair braided into a thick plait that reached halfway down her back greeted Alex warmly. "Hal caught a mess of salmon this morning," she said, "I set a couple aside for you. And we've got that rosemary bread you like, it came in on the noon boat." I bought a stuffed Orca whale for Rosie and we loaded the groceries into our bike baskets. On the way home we rode single file along a narrow road, and halfway there Alex stopped on a grassy verge." What's the matter?" I asked when I reached him. He was stretched out flat on the ground, his eyes closed.

"Nothing." He opened his eyes and pulled me down next to him. "I just realized I haven't kissed you in three hours." But when we got back on the bikes again he had me go first. When I looked over my shoulder, his seemed to be wobbling, and he dismounted just before we reached his driveway. "Tire must have a slow leak," he said. "I'll walk it the rest of the way."

"It looks fine to me."

"Until I put my weight on it. I'll put some air in it later."

That night we grilled the salmon and played a few hands of gin rummy before we went upstairs—in fact, we didn't even make it upstairs, not until later, after we'd made love on the leather couch. We took a long soak in the hot tub together—it had begun to rain, just a bit, and the clouds raced across the sky playing tag with the almost full moon. "So this is Northwest living," I sighed happily, leaning my head back against the rim of the tub so the jets could get the back of my neck. "Salmon, sex and suds. I could get used to this."

"That was the plan," he said.

"Well, it's working."

There was a lot of that kind of thing during the weekend—enough to make me think past the end of it, wonder, What's the catch? What's wrong with this picture? When does he turn out to be a serial killer or a closet conservative or a garden-variety asshole with a wife he forgot to tell me about? Because in my experience, limited though it may be, there's always something wrong with the picture.

Otherwise, I thoroughly enjoyed every minute of that weekend. It was so far from my real life—or what I thought of as my real life—that everything else receded into the background, not just the octopus but work, the kids, Rosie, my friends, everything that anchored me in the world.

We took a seaplane back to Seattle—Alex said he had a meeting at the cancer research center that morning, right next to the Lake Union Air dock, so it would be faster than flying his own plane and driving in from Boeing Field.

"I'll leave it on the island and catch the ferry up Friday—the weather map looks socked in next weekend, anyway," he said.

He put me in a cab at the Kenmore Air terminal, where we said goodbye.

"I had a wonderful time," I told him.

"The first of many," he promised. Then he leaned through the window and kissed me. "She's going to Sea-Tac," he told the driver, and strode off to his meeting.

He was right; I was, but not quite yet. First I had an appointment to keep with Dr. Kaplan.

CHAPTER
EIGHTEEN

Post-production is when you discover your mistakes, everything that somehow escaped your notice when you were writing or shooting your movie. It's when you realize that your mother was right—you should have gone to law school.

When we wrapped three weeks later and delivered the finished product, I cleared out my office. I was ready to go back to New York, but first I had to get a health certificate for Tory so I could take her on the plane.

"She's really slowing down in her old age, isn't she?" said the vet at the clinic in Westwood. I hadn't noticed it, but the young woman who'd taken over Dr. Wolfe's practice was right, she was. Not only that—she'd taken to peeing in the house occasionally, something she'd never done before, and she didn't jump up on my bed as easily as she once had, either. "When you get back to New York, you should take her to your regular vet for a check-up," she added.

Even New York's usual aggravations didn't dilute my happiness at being back: Go ahead, lady, cut in line, I don't care; No I don't mind standing here with my purchases while you file your nails; Of course I don't care if you seat me next to the kitchen, nobody wants to see a woman alone at one of the good tables, especially since everyone knows we're lousy tippers; That's fine, driver, just keep jabbering away on your cell phone while you barrel down Seventh Avenue at eighty miles an hour, isn't that a pedestrian you just ran over?

On a beautiful day in my favorite town in the best time of the year, when the trees on the block are in bloom and the kids from Omaha and Scranton in town for their graduation trips are taking pictures of each other in front of the memorial plaque at Strawberry Fields in Central Park, when the peonies come in at the Korean market on Amsterdam and soft shell crab at Empire Szechuan, I always think of that Irwin Shaw line about New York girls in pretty dresses, and am glad I'm alive.

I didn't even let the fact that the company that managed my building was going through its annual attempt to jack me out of my rent-stabilized lease dampen my spirits, although I had to go to landlord-tenant court, which is like the eighth circle of hell, to prove I still had a right to it, even though I owned property in another state. I won, but I knew if the show made it and I went back to California for more than a couple of weeks at a time the *goniffs* would try again, and might even succeed in forcing me out. (Lest you think that was a racial epithet and I am a self-hating Jew, I feel compelled to point out that the actual owners of the handful of rentals like mine and Mrs. B's are a couple of Hasidic brothers who have recently been indicted for money-laundering for the Columbian cartel).

Mrs. B. said it was my next-door neighbor who told the brothers I was hardly ever in residence. "I hear she wants your apartment," she said. "In the "F" line they're all one-bedrooms, very small, and she always has company, I see them coming and going at all hours."

While Mrs. B. knows a lot about what the tenants above the first floor read, she doesn't know much else about them, except the soap opera actress in 10A and the famous romance novelist in 6D. I, on the other hand, know exactly why Irina Marakova, she of the improbably yellow hair and carefully plucked eyebrows, has so many visitors; for years she's been running a totally unauthorized electrolysis practice out of her apartment, and paying off the super to keep quiet about it. So I retaliated by dropping a dime on her with the co-op board, which would likely earn me the eternal enmity of the super, but also meant I no longer had to hear the yelps of pain that came through my bedroom wall when Irina was depilating her clients, something I'd endured up to then in the spirit of good neighborliness and live and let live, as I told Alex when he came to my apartment for the first time.

I hadn't seen him in almost a month, which felt even longer now that I wasn't occupied with the show. He came to the city to meet with the mergers and acquisition companies that wanted to handle the sale of his company; he was busy during the days, but we spent nights and weekends together. He was a big hit with the girls—Peggy said he was far and away the most wonderful man I'd ever shown off, Carrie said he was like Big without the neuroses, and Suzanne said I shouldn't let myself get talked into a pre-nup.

Not that that ever came up. The subject of marriage, I mean. Mostly we just enjoyed being together and didn't talk about the future. I was content with what was happening between us—a gradual realization that we were very good together, that we were grateful and lucky to have found each other, and that I was happier than I ever remembered being.

"I think I've officially moved from pre-love formation to the real thing," I told Carrie.

"Has he?"

"It sure seems that way."

I felt better than I had since the first visit from the octopus, especially since if we got picked up for even a short season, I knew I had a long slog ahead of me.

"That sounds like just what you don't need," Dr. Kaplan had said when I saw him after my weekend in the San Juans with Alex. "In terms of your health, you're not doing any better than when you left the hospital—against my advice, if you recall. Your numbers haven't improved at all—you're still only around 50 percent."

"That's normal, though, right?"

"Just barely. In all honesty, I don't see how you can keep on doing what you're doing without drastically increasing your chances of having another event. It might not be the *takotsuba* the next time—it might be a major heart attack."

"How about a love affair? Wouldn't that be good for my heart?"

"That would depend on how stressful it is," he replied. "Studies show that the older people get, the more important emotional intimacy is for their overall well-being; there was an article about it in *JAMA* a few months ago."

"What about sexual intimacy?"

He smiled. "That's not bad for it, either. Once again, it depends—"

"I know, on how stressful it is," I interrupted him.

"Yes. Well, I'd like to keep monitoring you for another three months, but since you don't live here, I'll give you a referral in Los Angeles."

"One in New York would be helpful, too," I said. "And I may be coming back here—my life is sort of in flux now."

He wrote a couple of names on a prescription pad for me, made a slight change in my medication, and gave me the medical equivalent of fair warning: "You could be feeling fine one minute and dead the next," he said.

"Isn't that always the case? I mean, even if there's nothing wrong with you?"

He shrugged. "All I'm saying is, you're taking your life in your hands by continuing to work this hard." He was probably right, but if I couldn't work, I might as well be dead. It wasn't just the money—what really mattered was not being put out to pasture like a horse that can't race any longer. Television wasn't particularly significant or ennobling, but it was a world where I had a place—not at the top of the food chain, maybe, but a place nonetheless.

"Right," said Jessie when I said as much to her. "And they'll roll your name on the awards shows with all the others in the business who die during the year. Rosie and Zach and I will be sure to watch."

The networks wouldn't announce until the end of the month, so Alex and I decided to take a vacation. I lobbied for Paris—I'd never been there with a lover, and it stirred up all my romantic fantasies. But Alex wanted to go to the Caribbean. "We'll always have Paris," he said, doing a passable imitation of Humphrey Bogart.

"Yes, but Rick and Ilse already had it," I said.

"And so will we. But you'll love this place, I promise."

It was hard not to. It was one of those ultra luxe private hideaways developed by some Richard Branson wannabe that catered to the very rich and the very famous. I would drop some names if I could, but we hardly saw anyone when we were there except for Diane Sawyer and Mike Nichols, who nodded when they passed us on the beach, and a small family of the four most beautiful people in the world who looked like they'd stepped out of a Ralph Lauren "Home" ad. The service was of the appear-at-your-elbow-a-second-after-you-formulate-a-wish variety, and the food, the gardens, and the beach were spectacular.

The hotel had a little fleet of Lancers like the ones I'd learned to sail at summer camp, and when Alex insisted on racing me, I gave him a run for his money. We played tennis a few times although I was never very good at it and hadn't improved any with age. "We JAPS don't like sports where small projectiles fly at our faces at high speeds, especially if we've had our noses fixed," I told him.

"Have you?"

"Of course not, but the aversion is genetic, like Tay Sachs disease."

We swam and ate and made love, and everything was perfect until Alex announced that we were going scuba diving. "You don't have to be certified to try it," he said. "It's a resort course: the instructor shows you how to use the equipment and takes you down and stays with you every minute. And I'll be there, too."

"There is stuff in that ocean to whom I look exactly like dinner," I protested.

"These are fringe reefs on this island, we're in very shallow waters, there are no currents to attract big fish of any kind or nutrients in the water that would feed anything larger than a parrotfish," he replied. "There's never been a shark sighted within two hundred miles. It's like a huge coral garden swimming pool down there."

"What if the breathing thing doesn't work? What if I run out of air?"

"We won't go below one atmosphere—that's 33 feet. Even if you had a total equipment failure, which is highly unlikely, you could blow and go—one exhale and you're up, there's no excess nitrogen in your bloodstream to worry about, besides we can always buddy breathe, that's when you share your air with your dive partner— Sugar, don't give me that look, just try it. If you hate it you never have to do it again."

"Do I have to do it at all?"

"I'll be real sorry if you don't. But not as sorry as you will. It's an amazing world under water—you don't experience it the same way you do snorkeling. And you know how much you love that."

As we've already covered, physical bravery is not exactly my strong suit. Once I went rafting with some people I didn't know very well, and by the time we stopped to eat our lunch on the bank of the river, I'd had it. We weren't in killer rapids, but even so, I was frightened by the fast-moving white water. Even worse, I'd been stuck without a paddle, literally, in between a couple that fought the whole way down the river. "You promised me this was going to be fun, and it's not fun!" she whined, and even though I didn't particularly like her, she was saying what I would have said if I'd thought of it first. I decided I was far enough away from high school not to still have to play "Chicken!" and besides, back then I was practically the sole support of two minor children. After lunch I hiked out to the road and hitched a ride to the take-out spot where we'd left the car. The old man in the truck who picked me up said the river was exceptionally high and fast for that time of year, hadn't I seen the notices posted at the place we'd put in? Or heard about the raft that had capsized the day before? "They only found one body so far," he added ominously.

"Diving's absolutely the opposite of rafting," Alex said stubbornly. "You're not going fast, you're not out of control—two things I know you hate—and it hardly takes any effort at all. It's more like meditating than anything except climbing. And I know I'll never talk you into *that*."

"You've got that right," I replied. But I had to admit I was intrigued. Swimming was the only sport I was good at, the ocean was as warm as the pool, and I trusted Alex not to let anything bad happen to me.

It was thrilling. Scary, especially once my head was fully underwater and I was breathing through a mouthpiece, but it was so beautiful beneath the surface that my fear floated away with my air bubbles. It was a world Walt Disney might have dreamed up—a magic kingdom crowded with brightly colored fish with silly expressions on their faces and lacy coral fronds waving lazily in the barely noticeable current. Being weightless was amazing, especially when Genevieve, the pretty dive master, held my hands in hers while we did a tandem somersault in the water. She trailed behind Alex and me as we finned slowly along the wall of the reef, taking in the sights. He guided my index finger into the center of a gorgeous white-tipped purple anemone guarded by tiny orange striped clown fish, and I touched its quivering center for a half a second before it closed up, marveling at how soft and throbbing and alive it was; that night, when Alex whispered that I felt the same way, I guided his tongue to my clit and closed its lips around it with my fingers.

The next day I was eager to dive again—"You might as well get certified, as long as you're here," Alex suggested. Every day I felt more relaxed in the water, hovering nearly motionless above the reef while it revealed its secrets—a school of butterfly fish, a tiny sea horse clinging to an antler coral, nudibranks and French angels and a spiffy little fish I nicknamed Armani because it was midnight blue with neat white stripes on its dorsal fins. And just before we left the island, I let Alex talk me into doing a night dive.

"The reef is different at night," he told me. "The plants turn into animals and the animals turn into plants—you'll see." It was dusk when we got into the water; our headlights and flashlights intensified the colors of the reef's inhabitants as we sank into the increasing darkness.

The soft coral was alive with hungry little mouths, even formations that had looked like solid rock when we'd dived them that morning. Parrotfish dozed motionless in filmy, cobwebby cocoons spun out of their body; when larger fish approached, they snapped to attention like soldiers caught napping on parade, but once the danger was past they spun new ones and went back to sleep. A lobster swam out from its hole under a stand of stag horn coral that looked like a Georgia O'Keefe painting with water instead of desert in the background, blinking its beady little red eyes at us. And then an octopus floated in into view: trapped in my headlight, it looked even more startled than I was.

I took such a huge gulp of air I would have bobbed to the surface like a cork if Alex hadn't grabbed me and yanked me back down. He gave me the "are you okay?" sign, and when I nodded affirmatively, he looked relieved. The octopus didn't move at all—it stayed right where it was, regarding me through its slit-shaped eyes while I exhaled and concentrated on regulating my breathing, which sounded in my ears like a jet engine.

Nietzsche was right, I thought wildly—sometimes the abyss stares back. My heart probably didn't stop for more than a few seconds, but it wasn't until the octopus finally drifted away that it seemed to resume its normal rhythm. We hadn't been down very long, but by now it was fully dark and I was more than ready to get out of the water. I didn't want Alex to notice how panicky I was so I hugged my arms around my body, the signal for "I'm cold," and then pointed up. He nodded and we followed our bubbles slowly to the surface, where we struck out for the pier. At the ladder he took my fins and tank: "Are you okay?" he asked.

"I'm fine," I assured him. "I just got cold, I was ready to come up."

"I still have almost a full tank—would you mind if I went back down for a while?"

"Go ahead," I told him. "I'll see you back in the room."

That night I dreamed I was swimming underwater naked, without an air tank or a regulator. It was dark and deep and silent, but then I spied a pod of whales. They looked like Orcas, so transparent I could see right through their enormous bodies, which appeared to be lit from within. They paid no attention to me, even when I swam inside of them, where I floated in a formless void of white nothingness. I lingered there peacefully for what seemed a long time. I swam in, out and around them, trying to get them to notice me, even staring into their dark, lightless eyes, but they didn't blink. They were the universe, and I was nothing to them, so inconsequential I didn't matter. And then I woke up and reached for Alex in the darkness of our room.

We left the island the next day. As the plane rolled to a stop at Kennedy, Alex turned to me and said, "Whatever happens, I'll remember this trip for the rest of my life."

"What's all that about? Are you planning to scale Mt. Everest or fly into space or jump across the Grand Canyon on a motorcycle? Is there something you're not telling me?"

"Nothing like that," he said. "But you never know."

I only half-heard him—I was too busy listening to the messages on my cell phone from Sandro, Nelly and Robin. The network loved the pilot and had ordered six more episodes. My vacation was over.

CHAPTER
NINETEEN

The studio was fine for short visits but it was too small to live in for an extended period of time. Although the house needed a major overhaul, I settled for securing it against the next rainy season, which meant replacing missing roof tiles, fixing the gutters, and painting the faded stucco exterior.

Vaguely mission-style, the house had arched windows echoed inside by arched openings between the living room, dining room and kitchen—a mini-hacienda situated on a relatively flat half acre on the east side of the canyon overlooking the valley.

I hadn't inhabited it for more than a decade, and at first it felt like being the only remaining member of the original cast in a TV show that was a big hit in the beginning but ran its course after a few seasons. There were good memories in this house; we'd brought our babies back from the hospital to the sunny nursery, celebrated birthdays and anniversaries and Thanksgivings around the big oak table in the dining room, marked the kids' heights on the kitchen door as they grew, sat up late at night with friends who camped out in the spare room between jobs or deals or love affairs. But there were bad ones, too, like the night I got down on my knees and clutched

Ted's legs, begging him not to leave, or the morning I found a hundred dollar bill on the hall table, left there by a guy I brought home after he picked me up in the bar at the Beverly Wilshire the night my divorce was final—I'm still not sure which was the greater humiliation, having him believe I was a hooker or not thinking I was worth more than that. One day when I was putting groceries away I flashed on the day Ted got married again, when I sat down at the kitchen table and finished off two SaraLee cheesecakes by the time the kids got back from the wedding. I didn't stop stuffing my face until I'd gained thirty pounds—then suddenly one day it was over, as inexplicably as the time Paul stopped talking.

That was when Ted's father died; it wasn't until *shiva* was nearly over that we realized Paul hadn't said a word since the day his beloved *zaidie* collapsed on the sixth green at Hillcrest with a massive coronary. Years later, after Paul manifested his strange sensing ability too many times to chalk it up to coincidence, we finally figured it out: when Irv died, Paul, who was only five, probably felt his "thing" for the first time. It must have scared the words right out of him. The doctors were beginning to say that awful A word when he climbed into bed with us one night when I had a killer migraine and said, "Mommy, your head hurts me in mine," as clear as a piper's call. We made him say it again, and then sing us the whole alphabet song and recite *itsy bitsy spider*—when Ted muttered, "I'm going to sue those assholes," Paul giggled, and he went around saying it for days.

The house was full of memories like that, and as much as I'd once loved living in it, I knew that even if you could go home again, sometimes it was better not to. It was definitely time to move on. Once the show was on surer footing, I'd find a new place. Not a house, I didn't need all those empty rooms, but maybe a loft in some revitalized part of town or a condo on the beach where I wasn't surrounded by my past—at least, not the parts of it I'd just as soon forget.

Hallie started looking at real estate for me, even though I told her I was too busy to think about it. "I know what you need, I'll do all the prescreening and all you'll have to do is sign the check," she said. "The longer you wait, the more everything's going to cost."

"How much higher can prices get? Besides, I'm not going to see any serious money from the show for a while."

"So what? I could move this place tomorrow for close to two mil."

"You're kidding! The house isn't worth anything near that much."

"Maybe not, but the property is. A lot this size in this neighborhood? I've got two buyers who've been looking for a teardown around here for months. Even with capital gains tax, you could buy a fabulous apartment and have plenty left over."

I suddenly felt much more secure. "I'll think about it," I promised her. "Just let me get the show on the road first."

Making a series is much more difficult than shooting a one-off. Even though we weren't due to go on air until after the World Series was over, we had to have three episodes in the can by then and be rolling on the others. During the day I sat in endless meetings, saying yes, no and maybe to various requests and pitches. At night I ate takeout at the kitchen table and wrote, rewrote and edited. By the time I fell into bed at night, I was too tired to sleep: Instead, I stayed awake worrying about what I hadn't accomplished that day and why Alex was being so distant and uncommunicative.

He didn't drop off the radar entirely, but his phone calls and letters were brief and perfunctory—when we talked, he seemed preoccupied, although he said he wasn't, he was just tired. "I was in Houston for a few days," he said one night. "Went to see Chris."

"Really? What brought that on?"

"Oh, I guess I just figured it was time," he said. "Met his wife. A nice girl. She was a lot friendlier than he was. Evan came, too. He's always been easier than his brother."

"So you had a whole family reunion."

"Yeah, I guess you could say that."

"How come? Not that it's not a good thing, it is, but why now?" I asked.

"Why not?" he said, and changed the subject.

"Maybe he went to tell them about you," suggested Carrie.

"Then why wouldn't he have taken me along?"

"He could just be preparing them."

"For what? It's not like I'm moving in with them. Or him, either. Not yet, anyway."

That, like the M word, had never come up between us, which had been fine by me until now, when he was showing all the signs of a man backing away from a relationship.

"Or maybe he's just busy. You don't sell a big company in a few weeks, Sugar. Cut him some slack."

"I think he's losing interest," I told Suzanne a few days later. "I can always tell when a man's getting ready to dump me."

"No you can't," she said. "Remember that guy you were so sure was blowing you off when he stood you up the weekend we all went to New Orleans for the jazz festival? And then you found out he got run over on Madison Avenue?"

"He still could have called," I said. "They have phones in the emergency room."

"I wonder what I did wrong this time?" I asked Peggy.

"Why do you always think it was something you did?"

"Because it usually is and I usually do."

"That's ridiculous," she said. "Stop jumping to the wrong conclusions like you always do."

"Maybe I should get *caveat emptor* tattooed on my forehead. Or *abandon hope, all ye who enter here* on my snatch," I said glumly.

"Is that shtick or self pity?" she said. "It's entirely possible that there's something going on with him you know nothing about."

"Or someone," I said glumly.

"You don't have any reason to think that about him."

"I don't have any reason not to, either."

I could hear her sigh. "You're doing it again, aren't you?"

"Doing what?"

"Feeling like nobody could possibly love you, and then acting that way." Since Peggy got to be a life coach instead of a psychoanalyst, she's a lot more direct. "Welcome to managed care and skyrocketing malpractice," she said when she tossed out her couch. "I can't make a living doing analysis anymore. Besides, I hate waiting for my patients to get those moments of insight—they take so long and they're so infrequent. Coaching is much more efficient—you see what the problem is and tell them how to fix it."

"Just like that, huh?"

"Almost. Nobody's got time or money to relive their entire childhood any more. They just want to stop making the same mistakes over and over."

"And that's where you come in, huh?"

"Right-o-mundo."

Peggy doesn't try to shrink me, she just loves me—"Unworthy though you are," she says dryly—but when I'm stuck in my own *mishegas*, she does what she can to yank me out of the quicksand. "You always do the same thing when you think a man's planning to break up with you," she said that day "Premature evacuation."

"That's my line, get your own."

"Although I know it's hard for you to believe, much less consider, maybe it's not about you. Maybe you're the last thing on his mind right now."

"Is that supposed to be the good news? Because if it is, it doesn't make me feel any better."

It wasn't just that I was an emotional basket case—I wasn't feeling all that great either. You know how it is when the car develops a strange noise and you don't know what it is so you ignore it, and then there's another one, and you ignore that, too, but you get nervous every time you take it on the freeway, what if it just stopped or blew up during rush hour on the 405? That's what was happening to me. I fainted on the set once, and sometimes I asked Robin to take over because I had to go lie down in my office. There were a couple of mornings when I jut couldn't drag myself out of bed and make it to work. And more than once when I got to Jessie and Zach's house I couldn't summon up the strength to make it up the stairs, so I backed out of the driveway and went home.

I was pretty sure whatever was wrong could be cured by doing what Kaplan told me to: eat regular, well balanced meals, not hot dogs from Pink's on the way home or a couple of Krispy Kremes and a triple espresso before I got to the office; exercise every day, even though I left Laurel Canyon too early and when I got home it was too late and I was too tired to swim. And of course, best of all as far as Kaplan as concerned, quit my job.

That was a non-starter, even when I caught sight of myself in the mirror and wondered who that old lady in there was: It couldn't be me—inside, I was still a girl. Frances used to say "After a certain age a woman should only look from the neck down, otherwise she'll scare herself to death." When I turned 45 she said I shouldn't get on top anymore when I had sex with a man, so one night Hallie and I took the big gilt-framed mirror off her wall and set it on the coffee table. We looked down at our reflections and were horrified: "Oh shit," said Hallie,"she's right." Knowing Frances always was when it came to things like that; I made an appointment with a plastic surgeon the next day.

When I went for my physical for the insurance bond, I didn't mention my "condition," as Jessie insisted on calling it. Why bother—stress wasn't just a by-product of the job, it *was* the job, and if the network or studio found out about the octopus, they'd cancel my contract. At least I didn't have to wonder if the reason Alex was being so inattentive was that he didn't want a woman who *had* a condition—since few men would, especially someone who could be the poster boy for *Outside* or *Men's Health*, I hadn't gotten around to telling him about it yet.

If I could just get through the next few months, get the series running smoothly and picked up for a second season, I'd slow down and take care of myself, I promised the hag who lived in my bathroom mirror. Until then, I'd get pink bulbs for the light fixture.

"What about making Robin the show runner?" Jessie suggested. I hadn't noticed my daughter watching me from the top of the stairs as I struggled up them. We'd knocked off early that day, and I hadn't seen Rosie since she started cutting teeth. "You can't keep this up, Mom—it's killing you."

"Robin's good, but she's not that good," I said. "Besides, she's much too young for the job."

"That's ridiculous, she's almost as old as you were when you did *Going It Alone*. And you said yourself she saved the pilot."

"She stood in for me on the shoot for ten days. That's not the same thing as running a series."

"I stand corrected. The point is, you shouldn't be working this hard."

"No, the point is, if she takes over, what do they need me for?"

"Your ideas, your vision, your creativity. Why don't you just write the show and let her run it?"

Why not, indeed? It wasn't unheard of—plenty of the credits you see on TV series, the ones that say "created by," belong to the person who dreamed the show up, ran it for a season or two, and then went on to the next project. Sometimes they continued to write for their shows, even direct a few episodes, but once they tired of the daily grind they were happy to pocket a smaller piece of the action—which by anyone's standards except Hollywood's is still way above the poverty line—and do something else or retire to Palm Springs.

"Not yet," I said. "Maybe after the next show. Or the one after that."

CHAPTER
TWENTY

Once a series is up and running a show runner's like an air traffic controller. But before that it's more like being a test pilot—if there's a flaw in a part of a system or you're not paying attention, you can crash and burn. And I wasn't paying attention the way I should have been because Alex was taking up way too much room in my head.

I hadn't seen him in nearly two months—worse, even though he was calling more often these days, he never said he missed me or that he wanted to see me. And every time I thought about bringing it up, something stopped me—Frances' conditioning, no doubt.

"What is it you want?" asked Peggy.

I leaned back in my Aeron chair and stretched my legs out on the desk. "I want to *be* with him," I replied, louder than I realized until Robin, who was standing outside my office talking to one of the interns, craned her head in my direction to see who was in there with me. I waved her away and got up and closed the door.

"Then either ask for it or don't. Just don't expect me to keep listening to you bitch and whine about it," Peggy replied.

"Is that the way you talk to all your patients?"

"Damn straight. If I wanted to drown in their misery, I'd still be a therapist. But you're not my patient; you're my ridiculous girlfriend who still believes, deep down, that if she has to ask for something from a man, it's not worth having. Which is horse pucky, especially when the man is Alex. So either take the risk of being rejected—which is pretty slim, in my opinion—or shut up about it," she said, and hung up.

That night I called Alex and told him I missed him and I wanted to see him.

"I'm really glad to hear it," he replied, sounding happy and relieved at the same time, which was exactly how I felt. "I've missed you like crazy."

"You might have mentioned it."

"You said you were working like a lesbian. I don't know what that means, exactly—"

"It means you have to work twice as hard to get half as far," I said, "even in Hollywood where there are more gay women than anywhere in the country except maybe Northampton."

"I thought you didn't need any distractions."

"You're not a distraction," I said. "Well, you are, but in a good way. How does next week work for you? The show is shooting in Vegas, they can do that without me—should I come up there?"

"You sure you can get away?"

"Robin can handle it. I'll just tell them I'm taking some creative time—that's what writers say when they're doing anything else but putting words on paper. Getting grist for their mill."

"I'd be honored to be your grist. Or your grinder, even. How soon can you get here?"

I put in a one-day appearance on set in Vegas and then I took a bunch of incomplete scripts and outlines from the writing team as if I actually planned to work on them and flew to Seattle the first Tuesday in August. Alex and I were like two kids playing hooky from school—he checked in at the office by phone every day, the way I did with Robin, but mostly we forgot about work. We did the things tourists do in Seattle on those glorious days in midsummer they think about when it's snowing in Sheboygan or steaming in Orlando and they wonder why they don't just pack up and move west. We picnicked in the arboretum and the Japanese gardens, we swam in the Lake, we went to a Bonnie Raitt concert on the grounds of the Ste. Michelle winery, we cruised the Sound at dusk on an old fashioned tall ship and poked around the public market, where we watched guys in long white aprons toss salmon back and forth among themselves and play to the crowds that clapped and cheered them on. "They've been doing this act for a long time, they even wrote a motivational book about it," Alex said. "They made a presentation to us a couple of years ago for a team-building seminar they put on—they're big in the corporate training market, they probably make more money doing that than selling fish."

"Would you hire them?"

He snorted. "Not unless I owned a fish throwing team."

We went to the new public library I didn't get to see when I was in Seattle the last time because of the octopus and to a rock and roll museum that Frank Gehry designed for a software billionaire who spent a chunk of his fortune on his teenage obsessions—music, professional sports, rocket ships and science fiction. "He started Microsoft with Bill Gates," Alex told me. "Then he was diagnosed with a terminal disease, and he walked away from the company. When they cured it, he didn't want to go back. Instead, he did this, and a bunch of other crazy things."

"All his childhood fantasies come true," I said. "Like the character Tom Hanks played in *Big*."

"Was that a movie?" asked Alex, reminding me once again of how different our frames of reference occasionally were. Except for news and sports, he rarely watched TV, and he hadn't been to the movies in years. On the other hand, he read voraciously, books as well as newspapers, although he regularly threatened to cancel his subscription to the *New York Times*.

"I never thought I could be with a Republican," I said one morning when he was fulminating over a Paul Krugman column excoriating the administration's economic policy.

"Might that be a deal-breaker?" he asked good-naturedly.

"It would depend on the deal," I said. "Are you finished with the book review yet?"

One afternoon we went across the Sound to Port Townsend, where a couple from Texas who'd cashed in their options when Alex's first successful start-up paid off were raising two adopted little Chinese girls and restoring a graceful old Victorian house overlooking the harbor. I met some of Alex's other friends that week, too—the architect who'd designed his loft, a guy who hand-built custom kayaks and lived on a houseboat with a woman who restored old photographs and her teenaged son, the artist who'd done the Dalmatian coffee table. One day we had lunch with Kate, a lawyer Alex had mentioned a few times in that off-hand way that let me know there'd been something between them once. I could see why—she was quick, smart, and attractive, and they seemed to enjoy many of the same pursuits, like climbing and skiing and sea kayaking. She dropped a few references to places they'd done those things together but since she was getting married in September and invited me as well as Alex to the wedding, I liked her in spite of that. And when Alex offered his congratulations on her engagement, I couldn't detect even a hint of regret in his voice.

The only real disagreement we had that week was about my smoking. He was a terrible nag about it; once he said, "If I'd known when I met you that you were addicted to cigarettes, I'd never have—" but stopped before he finished the sentence. I didn't blow smoke in his face, or even light up in his presence, but the more open he was about his displeasure, the more pissed off I got. One night when I got into bed he sniffed audibly and said, "You smell like an ashtray."

"Oh, please—I had two drags a half hour ago, out on the deck. And I just brushed my teeth."

"Well, I don't want to sleep with you until you take a shower and wash your hair."

"Why don't I just go to a hotel?" I replied hotly.

"Suit yourself," he said and turned over.

I stared at his back for a while, and then went for a long walk, smoking every step of the way until I was dizzy and my throat was raw. When I went back to the loft, hoping to find Alex pacing the floor worrying about me, he was fast asleep, which made me even madder. I slept in the other bedroom; when I woke up the next morning, Alex was gone. He'd left a note in the kitchen next to the coffeemaker: "Had to go to the office to sign some papers—back before noon. Hope you slept well."

We didn't talk about it again, and that night when he unwrapped the short silk kimono I wore to bed he had the good sense not to say anything about the nicotine patch on my right breast.

Except for that, it was a wonderful few days, different from the island or even our time together in New York—more real, in a way. Seattle wasn't New York, or even L.A., but it was easy to imagine living here, and being happy. Not now, but maybe some day.

It was over a month before we got together again. He came to L.A. for a weekend, but it wasn't until I picked him up at the Ontario airport that I realized he'd flown his own plane down.

"Are you nuts? The weather's awful—it's been this way for days, nothing but wind and rain from here to there. Why didn't you fly commercial?"

"I've flown through a lot worse," he said, more jauntily than he looked; his face was pale and he was moving more slowly than usual. "Besides," he added, managing a grin, "what's life without risk?"

I steered us onto the freeway, enjoying the throaty hum of my new wheels, a sporty little red Lexus convertible the studio had leased for me. Alex dozed most of the way home: "Sorry," he mumbled as I pulled into the driveway, "I didn't get much sleep last night."

I showed him around the house, which had been smartened up a bit at Hallie's urging: "You want to be ready to put it on the market by spring," she said, and when I protested that I didn't have time, she got the women who stage her real estate listings to do it all for me; I went on location with the show for a week, and when I came back, the place looked too nice for a tear-down. "It's just paint, plants, window treatments and a couple of coats of Swedish finish on the floors," she said. "Nobody who can afford it would actually live in it the way it is—no offense, but if they didn't tear it all the way down they'd probably gut it. Don't think of this as redecorating, just the first step in marketing."

It was still enough to invigorate my nascent nesting instinct. Before Alex came down I ordered a new mattress and spent an hour at Bed Bath and Beyond picking out new bed linens. The day of his arrival I got up early and marinated the lamb in olive oil, mustard, rosemary and garlic, made a leek and onion tart, peeled some little new potatoes and set the table. By the time we ate he looked better, but he only picked at the dinner, and a couple of times he excused himself to use the bathroom. "It must have been that burrito I ate coming down," he said.

The rain had stopped so we took Tory for a walk before we turned in. She was moving very slowly and she stumbled a lot: I told Alex about my conversation with her vet before I left New York. "He said her heart's slowing down, that's why she pants so much. And she's pretty blind—see how cloudy her eyes are? Right now she doesn't seem to be in any pain, but he said I needed to prepare myself for when I have to put her down."

My eyes filled with tears again the way they had in Dr. Rosen's office. "How do you prepare yourself for that?" I asked Alex. "I've buried a couple of goldfish, a cat and a hamster, but I couldn't stand losing Tory—she's part of me."

"What if she couldn't control her bodily functions? What if she didn't even recognize or respond to you any more? Could you let her go then?"

"As long as she wasn't suffering, I'd keep her alive as long as I could. When you love someone as much as I love her, every day's a gift," I told him.

The next morning Alex was feeling better and we christened the new bed properly, not once but twice. We went to a polo match at Will Rogers' ranch in Santa Monica that afternoon—it was a benefit for one of Nelly's pet causes and I'd been guilt-tripped into spending $500 for a pair of tickets, but I got to show Alex off, which made up for it. On Sunday we went to Jessie and Zach's for brunch—Paul came, too, the first time I'd seen him in almost a month. There was a time when my kids didn't like each other, or so it seemed to me then, but that ended a few years ago, which relieved me no end—as Frances used to say, and still does, "When I'm gone all you'll have is each other," which isn't true: Jessie has Zach and one of these days Paul will find a nice girl and marry her, but when I point that out to my mother, she says it's not the same thing: "If God forbid one of them needed a kidney, they couldn't get it from a husband or wife, only a sister or brother." Needless to say, my mother's worst-case scenarios are bleaker than mine—that was one I'd never considered.

Regardless, I was glad my children had grown to appreciate each other, and that they both seemed to like Alex. As we left the house in Echo Park, Jessie stage-whispered, "I think he's a keeper, Mom," and Paul said, "That goes for me, too."

That night Hallie had us over for dinner, and we ate and drank and talked and laughed until I realized it was nearly midnight and I had to work the next day. On the way home I sighed.

"What was that about?" Alex asked.

"Just the Sunday night dwindles. I wish you didn't have to go home tomorrow and I didn't have to go to work."

"Then don't. Come with me."

"I wish I could, but there's the little matter of this job I have. I won't have another free day until forever—Christmas, at least. And then if we go to a full season, a week at the most before it starts all over again."

"Have you ever thought about chucking it?"

"In the last couple of months? At least once a day."

"So why don't you? Think of all the places you've never been! We could go to Africa for the migration on the Serengeti; I've always wanted to do that. Or get a house for a couple of months in Bali—they say it's beautiful. And we could go to Paris in the spring—I said I'd take you there, didn't I? Let's do it!" His eyes danced with excitement—he was as enthusiastic as a boy.

"And how would I fund this extravaganza, out of my unemployment check?"

"I've got enough money for both of us," he said carelessly. "It would be great...Sugar, say yes. Please. You won't be sorry, I promise."

"Oh, Alex, you know I can't. It would be wonderful, but there's just no way, not now. Maybe Paris in the spring, though—I'd like that."

And that was where we left it. I lay awake after he fell asleep, thinking about what it would be like to wake up next to him every morning, spend weeks and months with him in all the places I'd always dreamed of seeing with someone I loved. And I did love Alex Carroll—if I hadn't been certain before, I was now. But romance is all about timing, isn't it? And right then, I had hardly any to spare.

I was curled up in his arms when he fell asleep, and after a while Tory got up on the bed and stretched out her body next to me. Sandwiched between them, I fell asleep, my backside tucked into Alex's and my fingers buried in her soft curls. Sometime just before dawn I woke up from a dream about Uncle Max. We were driving in his jaunty little roadster along a winding road down the side of a mountain, with a rice paddy on one side and the sea on the other. We pulled up alongside a wizened old man in black pajamas and a coolie hat, coaxing a flock of ducks across the road and into the paddy with a bamboo pole. We stopped and Uncle Max handed me a Polaroid camera like the one he gave me on my twelfth birthday. "It's not the things you do you regret later, it's the ones you don't," he said, and when I got out of the car he rolled up the windows and locked the doors. Then he drove away, straight into the ocean, while the ducks took to the air with a noisy thwack of their wings.

It began to rain, a cold, drenching downpour, and I woke up to discover that Tory had peed all over the bed.

Alex was great about it—he helped me strip the bed and change the sheets, and when I started to cry, he didn't ask why, just held me and stroked my hair until I fell asleep again.

CHAPTER
TWENTY-ONE

Alex came down again a few weeks later for Thanksgiving. He asked if it would be okay to include his son Evan, who arrived in Echo Park with a pretty half-Asian girl named Lee whom he introduced as a friend from work.

Evan didn't resemble Alex at all. He was slight and fair, with longish blonde hair and pale eyes, and seemed quiet and even shy at first, but when he and Jessie started taking about music, he grew lively and animated. "Some buddies of mine and I have a band," he explained. "Kind of an alt rock sound. We started playing together in grad school. We get a few gigs here and there—we call ourselves Last Kid Picked."

"Because you all used to be science nerds?" I asked.

"Still are," he said. "We're playing at Spaceland next week—Dad, you won't be here, but the rest of you ought to come. That is, if you want to."

"I might," Jessie said. "Spaceland, huh? That's quite a coup."

What's Spaceland?" Alex asked.

"It's a club in Silver Lake," she explained. "They book a lot of indie acts just before they break out. Beck used to play there and so did the Black Keys. Your group must be pretty good."

"We have a good time," Evan said with a modesty I found becoming as well as real, a rarity in this town, especially among the young. "But nobody's quitting their day job any time soon."

"Would you, if you could?"

"Doubtful," he replied. "I'd rather study the stars than be one. Besides, I'm applying for the astronaut program. I know it's a long shot, but like you used to say, Dad, there's no percentage in playing the short ones."

I saw the look of pleasure flit across Alex's face.

"I know a couple of people who are pretty high up in NASA. Want me to put in a word?" he asked his son.

"Uh...I don't think so. I mean, that's really nice of you, but I'd rather you didn't. Not now, anyway."

Later I said, "How come you asked him? Why didn't you just call whoever you know and do it?"

"Is that what you'd do?"

"Probably not if it meant my kid would climb into a contraption built by the lowest bidder and blast into the stratosphere. But generally speaking, sure. If I had the juice that would help them get ahead, I'd use it."

"Even if they didn't want you to?"

I shrugged. "So you apologize later, big deal. They'd get over it, especially if they got what they wanted."

"Even if then they felt like they didn't make it happen, you did?"

"That probably wouldn't have occurred to me."

"I'm surprised," he said. "I mean, given what you've told me about your mother."

Now it was my turn to be surprised. "You're right, you know. Are you always this smart?"

"Not all the time. But I'm a good listener. Which reminds me—when do I get to meet the redoubtable Frances?"

"One of these days," I said airily. In fact, I hadn't even made my mother aware of Alex Carroll's existence. That way, if this relationship ended up like all my other ones, I wouldn't have to hear her tell me it was my entire fault.

As much as I wanted to spend the whole weekend with Alex, I couldn't. We had three more episodes to wrap before Christmas, so I sent him home Friday morning and went back to work. He called me a few days later. "I've got an offer you can't refuse," he said. "I've rented a house in Vail from Christmas through New Year's. Chris and his wife are coming—did I tell you she's pregnant? And so are Evan and his girlfriend. I want you and your kids to come, too. They all ski, right?"

"Everybody except me."

"I'll teach you. Or you can hang out with Rosie while we're skiing. Or we'll hire a sitter and you can do whatever you want. There's plenty of room for everyone. And I chartered a plane, so you can all come together. You can bring Tory, too."

"Wow—you do things in a big way, don't you? I don't know what to say. I don't even know if Zach can take that much time off."

"He said the restaurant business is dead that whole week, it shouldn't be any problem. He already checked with Paul—he's coming too."

"You seem to have it all figured out."

"You're not mad, are you? I wanted to surprise you. Wait—you don't already have plans for New Year's Eve, do you?"

I hadn't had plans for New Year's Eve since the last time I could remember, unless you count reserving *Now Voyager*, and *The Way We Were* at Blockbuster in case every other dateless woman in town hadn't already rented them.

"I'm sure George Clooney can find another date," I told him, and somehow I found time the week before we wrapped the show for the holidays to buy gifts for everyone. I wasn't sure about Alex's sons, so I chose ski goggles for them, silk scarves for Chris's wife and Evan's girlfriend, a set of expensive Japanese knives for Zach and a red leather jacket for Jessie. I splurged on Rosie—a humongous stuffed St. Bernard, a string of baby pearls

I'd add to as she got older, a darling little smocked dress and a bright yellow snowsuit. Paul got new ski boots as well as goggles, and I tucked in an extra scarf because he said Kelly was coming, too. "And no giving her the third degree, Mom," he warned.

"I'll try to restrain myself."

He snorted. "Restraint is not a concept you're familiar with."

He was right. When Alex and I went to an exhibit of Eugene Atget photographs at the ICP in New York, he'd lingered over an image of a Paris street at dawn, so when I found a vintage print of it by Berenice Abbott in a gallery on Melrose, I bought it for him, even though it cost more than all my other purchases combined. But I was feeling pretty flush, given the way the show was shaping up and also Hallie's estimate of how much my house was worth. Jessie met me at the Beverly Center the night before we left and we bought red felt Christmas stockings for everyone, along with tangerines, wind-up toys, little electronic gizmos, disposable cameras, ski socks and ribbon candy—"It's great, there are no baggage limits on private planes," she said happily.

There aren't crowds of holiday travelers jamming the security lines either, or center seats, cranky flight attendants or stale peanuts. And you can bring your dog in the main cabin, too. Alex had thought of everything—he'd sent a limo as long as a city block to pick us all up, and even before takeoff the stewardess brought the grown-ups mimosas, a tippy cup of apple juice for Rosie, and doggy treats for Tory. As soon as we were aloft breakfast was served on real plates with heavy silver utensils—warm croissants, deviled eggs topped with caviar, strawberries with Devonshire cream, and coffee poured from a French press pot. "I feel like a movie star," Jessie said. "Mom, you'd better not fuck this up."

"I'll try not to," I assured her.

Alex met us at the Eagle County airport in Vail, which was crowded with Lear Jets, Gulfstreams, and a couple of 737's. We climbed into another limo; he had more champagne waiting, and I accepted a glass—after all, I wasn't driving. "It doesn't get much better than this," I told him happily.

"Oh, yes it does," he said. "Just wait and see."

The house was your basic ten million dollar ski lodge, complete with Jacuzzis in every bathroom, fireplaces in all the bedrooms, a fleet of Range Rovers, SUV's and Snowmobiles in the garage, and a cook, maid and driver. It belonged to a wealthy Texan who'd backed Alex's first company. "Fortunately, he never held that against me, and lucky for us, his wife likes their place in St. Bart's better," Alex said.

While I unpacked and hung up my clothes, including the sexy black backless dress I'd bought for New Year's Eve, Alex stretched out on the bed in our room. I took a satisfying soak in the tub and crawled in next to him; sex is better before dinner than after, you don't feel like such a stuffed pig or make those embarrassing noises as the meal makes its way through your digestive system. I was also very horny—it was three weeks since the last time we'd made love. That's the thing about sex—when it's not a regular part of your life you stop missing it eventually, especially when you're past the age when your hormones do the thinking for you. All mine were on full alert, and I used my tongue and fingers as enticingly as I knew how, but I couldn't rouse him, so I closed my eyes, and the next thing I knew, Jessie was tapping on the door to tell us dinner was ready.

When we came downstairs, Evan was fooling around at the Steinway in the great room; he banged out a chorus of "We're the Brady's," which everyone sang amid much laughter. The week after Thanksgiving, Jessie'd gone to hear his band at Spaceland: "They're really, really good," she said, "They've got a great sound. Of course, they're science guys, they don't know anything about the music business, but with the right management, they could go places."

"Are you going to rep them?"

"I'm tempted," she said. "We're talking about doing something together—we'll see."

"I thought you didn't want to go back to work until Rosie's in preschool."

"I don't—not full-time, anyway. I'm happy being a mom, but frankly, I miss being back in the world with grownups. Not that most of my clients are, but you know what I mean."

Love and work, career and family—it's the same old story, no matter how equal we are, we're the ones who have to choose between them. "It's always a balancing act, isn't it?"

"At least you don't have to deal with that any more."

Not this week, at least. I'd turned off my cell phone when the car picked me up, not even bothering to return the calls from Nelly and Sandro. They probably just wanted to wish me a merry Christmas, and it looked as though I had that covered.

Alex's older son Chris looked exactly like him, right down to the set of his jaw. There was no warm fuzzy vibe between the two men—they seemed more like two boxers feeling each other out than father and son. It wasn't until we sat down at the table and Alex said. "Chris, would you say grace? I think we all have a lot to be grateful for tonight" that he seemed happy to be there, and Angela, his wife, shot Alex a look of relief. Alex had told me they were evangelical Christians, very active in one of those mega churches that seemed to be the center of their life. "They dragged me there when I was in Houston," he said.

"Did you get saved?" I teased. We were in bed, and I was blissfully post orgasmic.

"Yep, when I met you," he said, squeezing my ass. "Seriously, they seem to get a lot out of their faith. In a way I envy them. If you believe there's a heaven, and you're going there, death's no big deal. It's Pascal's wager—if you gain, you gain all, and if you lose, you lose nothing. It's basic decision theory—that is, if you think the question of whether God exists is worth considering."

"Do you?"

"Not when there's something else to think about. Like this," he said, his lips moving down my body to where his fingers were. Then he did that thing I loved, spooning out my pussy juices with his fingers and rubbing them all over my breasts and belly before licking them off. "Pascal, huh?" I said sleepily later. "Just what I always dreamed of...a fucking philosopher."

I'd talked to Kelly a little on the plane, but I sat her next to me at dinner so I could get to know her better. This was the first time in years Paul had introduced me to a girl, which might mean it was serious. They say men marry some version of their mother, but Kelly was slender and fine-boned, with green eyes, red hair and freckles, as Irish as her name—also unlike me, she didn't talk unless she had something to say. She came from San Francisco—I gathered they had more kids than money, or else they were extremely patriotic, because like her four brothers, who'd gone from high school right into the military, she'd gotten her nursing degree on the Army's dime and then served in Iraq and Afghanistan.

She worked in the ER at St. John's in Santa Monica, which was how she'd met Paul. "He brought in a guy from his building site that fell off a ladder and said he was fine, but Paul didn't think so," she said. "He was right—the guy didn't have any serious injuries from the fall, but we did a head scan anyway and it turned out he had something else wrong—a tumor that, thanks to Paul, they think they got in time." Her eyes shone with admiration, or maybe it was love. "He's really tuned into people—it's like he's got a sixth sense when there's something wrong with them, you know?" Jessie and I exchanged glances across the table—yes, we knew. "He's going to make a wonderful physician's assistant, don't you think?" Kelly went on. Next to her, Paul squirmed and looked sheepish.

"Terrific," I agreed, wondering if there were other secrets my son was keeping from me. You think you know your kids, but you don't, really—you only know who they used to be, when you knew everything about them or thought you did.

After dinner Evan played Christmas carols and we sang until the baby began to fuss and Jessie took her upstairs. The men settled down to watch a football game on the big plasma TV in the library, the girls said they had presents to wrap, and I stretched out on the couch with a new Dennis Lehane novel.

Around eleven o'clock Angela and Chris announced that they were going to midnight services in the village. "Anyone else want to come?" Chris asked.

"I think I will," said Alex. "Sugar?"

"No, you go ahead. I'm going out for a little fresh air and then I'm turning in—it's been a long day."

I wanted him to be alone with them, and I wasn't big on church anyway, so I went outside after they left to have the one cigarette I hadn't been able to give up—well, maybe the second or third—when Paul joined me. "Guess I should have told you, huh?"

"Any reason why you didn't?"

"I wanted to make sure I was accepted first."

"When do you start?"

"In January. It's a two-year program at USC. That day I met Kelly when I brought Brent in, and the next time I saw her when she told me about his tumor—it got me thinking, I have this thing, maybe I should do something useful with it."

"I thought it only happened with us."

"So did I. Maybe it wasn't—you know, my thing. Maybe it was just a coincidence."

I raised an eyebrow. "Have you sensed anyone else lately?"

"Sort of. Not really. With Kelly once, when she...well, when she had a miscarriage. She didn't even know she was pregnant yet."

I didn't ask what the circumstances of that misconception were, but Paul looked sad, and I squeezed his hand. "Rosie would have had a cousin," he said.

"When the time is right, she will have," I replied. "With anyone else?"

"I'm not sure. It can be hard to tell." He plucked the cigarette out of my fingers and stubbed it out in the snow. "You don't really want that," he said.

"Yes, I do—I did," I replied. "What do you think of Alex?"

"He seems like a great guy, and obviously he's seriously crazy about you. Do you love him?"

"As a matter of fact, I do."

"Then I'm glad for you, Mom. Take good care of each other, okay?"

"I intend to."

The next morning we opened presents. Evan gave us all CD's of his band, and Chris's wife had knitted mittens for everyone, even Rosie. Paul made me a beautifully inlaid jewelry box and Jessie gave me a red leather jacket almost exactly like the one I'd bought her—"You shouldn't have!" we exclaimed, and every time we wore them that week we giggled.

Alex had gone all out—new snowboards for his sons, iPods for Zach and Paul, a video recorder for Angela—"for when the baby comes," he said—perfume for the girls, and a silver Patagonia ski parka for Jessie. He handed me a small blue box and I held my breath as I opened it. Inside was a pair of square-cut emerald earrings that flashed with light.

"They're beautiful, Alex. I love them." I meant it—they were exquisite. But as soon as I saw the box from Tiffany my heart gave a little thump. Was it a ring? Here, now, in front of everyone? And if it was, what would I say?

"They reminded me of that silky thing you wore that first night, remember?" he murmured as I fastened them in my ears.

"I remember," I said, kissing him. Besides, even if he did propose, I couldn't marry him. The show wasn't a sure thing yet. And I hadn't I told him about the octopus, which would very likely write "finis" to any ideas he might have along those lines.

Since the staff was off for the holiday Zach had volunteered to cook Christmas dinner. They'd left us everything we needed, including a turkey, and before the kids left for the slopes, he stuffed it and slid it into the oven. "Don't forget to baste it," he said as he went out the door.

"I was cooking turkeys before you were born," I said scornfully.

"But not nearly as well," said Jessie.

Chris's wife wasn't quite past the first trimester and she'd had one miscarriage already, so she stayed behind with Rosie and me while everyone else headed for the slopes. We did the breakfast dishes and looked in the cupboards and refrigerator to see what else the staff had left us in besides the turkey. "Oh, good, everything we need for pies, should we make them?" asked Angela.

"Why not?" I peeled and sugared the apples while she rolled out the dough on the granite counter. We worked in companionable silence, Rosie crooning to herself in the Johnny Jump-Up.

When I brought it out, Jessie was dubious. "They don't use those anymore, they say it keeps them from trying to walk, where did you ever find it?"

"In a box of your old baby clothes in the basement. You and Paul used to love it. And you were both walking before you were a year old. Believe me, when she starts cutting her molars you'll be glad you have it."

"You can't tell my mother anything," Jessie said to Angela when I hung up the sling and set Rosie inside it. Her chubby little legs dangled from the faded canvas seat and she gave an experimental bounce.

"She does seem to like it, though," Angela said as Rosie bounced some more and crowed with laughter.

"Don't encourage her, the next thing you know she'll be getting you one."

"My mother already did," Angela replied, and they giggled like coconspirators.

We made two pumpkin and two apple pies, and then we fed Rosie and took her outside. "It's beautiful here," Angela said. "I'm glad we came. At first Chris didn't want to, but..."

"I'm glad you did, too. It means a lot to Alex."

"To Chris too, even though he won't admit it. Especially now."

"You mean, with the baby coming?"

She gave me an enigmatic look. "That and...other things."

I didn't ask what she meant—for once, Sugar, mind your business, I thought. "They're a lot alike, you know, Chris and Alex," I said. "Straightforward, sure of themselves—"

"Stubborn," she added. "Maybe that's why things are hard for them. I hope they sort them out before..."

"Before what?"

"uh...before the baby's born. Did Chris tell you we're going to name it after his father? Alex if it's a boy, Alexandria if it's a girl."

Jews believe it's bad luck to name a baby after a living person, but I didn't mention that; as Evan had said the night before when Chris and Alex argued about the war in Iraq, "This is a purpose-driven vacation, bro, and the purpose is fun, so no politics or religion, okay?"

It was a clear, cold sunny day—perfect weather for skiing if you like that sort of thing, or playing in the snow if you're nine months old and you've never seen or tasted it before. Jessie came home to give Rosie lunch and put her down for a nap, so I went for a walk, past the line of aspens at the back of the property and through the brushy woodland that got thicker and denser as it wound up toward the mountain. I followed a trail through the woods for a quarter of a mile or so. The rise was gradual, the quiet absolute—there was something almost spiritual about the way the trees made a canopy over my head.

Suddenly the quiet was shattered by a loud thrashing noise, which was followed a heartbeat later by a deer that leaped out of the brush less than five feet from where I stood. His hooves flashed in front of my eyes as he bounded past me and disappeared into a thick stand of trees. I was so startled it seemed like my heart had come loose from its moorings and was trying to get out of my chest; first I felt a short, sharp pain and then I felt so dizzy I sat down in the middle of the path until the adrenaline rush receded and I could stand up again. That's all it was—Generalized Arousal Syndrome, as Dr. Kaplan had explained, better known as the fight-or-flight response. It didn't exactly cause my *takutsoba*, but it was what he called a precipitant. Except for work, I'd tried to avoid adding any new stress to my life, which I considered before I let Alex talk me into diving. But I did it anyway. I'd been fine underwater until I saw the octopus, and I'd lived through that, hadn't I?

I'd live through this, too. I willed the hormones to go back where they came from and take the octopus with them. *Octopus, octopus go away, come again some other day* played in my head all the way back to the house like an advertising jingle you can't forget. Before much longer, I knew, I'd have to tell Alex about him.

CHAPTER
TWENTY-TWO

Zach came back from the mountain after a couple of runs and took over in the kitchen. The rest of us were sniffing and tasting when Alex and his sons came in.

"How was it?" I asked

"Incredible!" said Evan. "We went to Golden Peak, they have this amazing superpipe—you should have seen us whizzing up and down those twenty foot walls. We got Dad on a board, and he did pretty good, considering."

"Don't patronize your old man, kid," said Alex, shaking the snow off his parka and planting a chilly kiss on my head.

"I wasn't being patronizing, it's like I told you—boarding's not like skiing. Your center of gravity's lower, and the balance is different—that's probably why you kept falling."

"I didn't keep falling, it was only twice. Tomorrow we're hitting the Exterminator—you can ride your board, but I'll be leaving my tracks in your powder."

Chris looked worried. "Dad, do you think that's such a good idea? It's a double-diamondback, maybe we just ought to cruise Big Bowl instead."

"Why, you chickening out? If memory serves, the first time you skied that run, it was with me."

"Yeah, but that was a long time ago, before—" He looked at me and stopped.

"Before what?" I asked. "Is it really called the Exterminator? Alex, maybe Chris is right, maybe it's not such a good idea."

"It'll be fine, Sugar, don't worry," he said, but he didn't answer my other question.

By the time we finished dinner, everyone was Chrstmassed out—the kids were nodding out, Rosie had a meltdown and refused to be soothed, and pretty soon they drifted away from the table and disappeared upstairs.

I wrapped the leftover turkey in aluminum foil, covered the remains of the pies with Saran wrap and started to load the dishwasher, but Alex stopped me. "Leave it," he said.

"I can't leave dirty dishes in the sink at night. When I try to, I get up at three a.m. and wash them so I don't have to face the mess in the morning," I protested.

"Another of Frances's Rules?"

I thought for a minute. "Probably. We always had to clean up after her parties. My father used to bring her breakfast in bed every morning before he went to the office. When I got married, she said I should ask Ted to do it, right away, while the bloom was still on the rose—"She used to say, 'The way you start out is the way you end up.'"

"I'd tell you the staff will do it tomorrow, but it wouldn't make any difference, would it?" he said. It was one of the things I liked about Alex—he knew which battles were worth fighting.

He found a bottle of armagnac among the array of liqueurs on the open steel shelves that hung over the long expanse of granite that bisected the enormous kitchen, which Zach said was better than the one in his restaurant—"A million five, easy," he estimated enviously.

"So did you? Did Ted bring you breakfast in bed every day?" Alex asked.

"Hardly," I said. "But he had this thing about wanting to have his shirts freshly ironed when he went to court, so I did it, even though I hate to iron. My parents were visiting us once, right after we were married, and Frances saw me doing it—she was horrified." I laughed out loud, remembering. "She said, just burn it, he'll never ask you to iron his shirts again. She was right, of course—after the second time I did it, he started taking them to the French laundry."

This is how intimacy comes later in life, without the accretion of years of knowing someone, of a shared history—in moments when long-forgotten fragments of the past surface and suddenly you're talking about something that happened so long ago you barely remember who you were then. (Or, as Suzanne once said, men don't just love younger women because they're beautiful, it's because their stories are shorter.)

Alex poured us a couple a snifters of the brandy and perched companionably on a stool while I washed the wine glasses by hand—they were Tiffany crystal like the ones one of Ted's rich clients gave Jessie and Zach when they got married. She never puts hers in the dishwasher, so I didn't, either. When the kitchen was close enough to spotless so the staff wouldn't think we were slobs, Alex and I curled up on one of the leather couches that were grouped around the circular fireplace in the great room in an attempt to make it look less like the lobby of a hotel and more like people actually lived there. Unlike the fireplaces in the bedrooms, this one was gas-powered, and appeared to burn perpetually with a cool blue flame.

"So what did you do all day while I was getting my ass kicked by my kids on the mountain?"

"Read, hung out, made pies with Angela, took care of the baby, went for a walk in the woods behind the house. I almost got run over by Bambi."

He cocked an eyebrow at me quizzically.

"This deer jumped out of the brush right in front of me and scared the hell out of me." I took a deep breath. "Alex, there's something I have to tell you."

"Go ahead. I'm listening."

"After that first time I came to Seattle, on the way to Vancouver when I stood you up for lunch...well, I didn't really stand you up. I mean, I did, but it wasn't because there was an emergency on the set. The emergency happened before that."

"When you collapsed at the bookstore."

"Yes, when I ...how did you know about that? Did Paul tell you? Or was it Jessie?"

"Neither one of them. I stopped in at the café a week or so later and heard about how Heidi saved some woman's life. She didn't know it was you, she just said it was—" He hesitated.

"It was what?"

"Umm...'some old lady' I think was the way she put it. Don't look so horrified, Sugar, she's just a kid, anyone over 30 looks old to her. Me, too. She tried to fix me up with her mother once."

"Did you go?"

"Of course not." He looked annoyed. "Anyway, I came in again a few days later, and she said, you know that woman I was telling you about? We found her keys in a little leather case that must have dropped under the stairs when she fell. There was a business card inside it, she said, some tourist from California." He smiled. "I think her exact words were, 'with that mouth on her, I was sure she was a New Yorker.'"

"So she told you my name?"

"No, why would she? She didn't know I knew you."

"You just recognized me from that brilliant description, huh? An old lady from California with a big mouth?"

"Shouldn't I have?"

His voice was teasing, but his eyes were serious, and locked onto mine like a laser—I squirmed uncomfortably under his scrutiny. This was not the way I'd planned this conversation. I was going to start out with something funny, like, "Did I ever tell you about the time I was attacked by the Killer

Sushi?" and then maybe segue into explaining that I didn't tell him when it happened because I didn't want him to worry.

"The next day I got your e-mail, so I called you at the hotel in Vancouver. When they said you hadn't checked in yet, I put it together," Alex continued,

"So you knew I'd lied to you."

He shrugged. "Everybody's got secrets. And their own reasons for keeping them. I figured when you were ready to tell me, you would. Or not."

"I guess this would be a good time, right?" And then I did: Sugar and the Octopus, the unexpurgated version.

He listened intently, interrupting only when I insisted it hadn't been a heart attack.

"So this thing you had, this *takotsubo*—it's caused by emotional stress, right?"

"Well, yes but—"I began.

"And you're going back to L.A. and write and produce a whole season of shows between now and May, right?"

"Not all by myself, I've got a writing team and a bunch of AP's, and Robin, and—"

"I see," he said evenly.

Sometimes his eyes were so purple they were almost black. This was one of those times. "No, you don't see, not really. Look, Alex, this is what I *do*. It's who I *am*."

He got up and topped off his brandy snifter. "I understand, Sugar. Believe me, I really, really get it," he said. "But did you not tell me because you thought it would change how I feel about you?"

"I don't know," I said in a very small, quiet voice. "I don't know how you feel about me."

"You don't?" He looked incredulous.

I shook my head—after all, he'd never come right out and said the words.

His face darkened. "Well, when you figure it out, let me know," Then he stood up, took his parka from the clothes tree in the foyer, put it on and went out the door.

He didn't come back until after midnight. I'd already gone up to our room when I heard a car drive up and then the sound of the front door opening and closing again. I lay awake for a long time until I realized he wasn't going to join me so I swallowed a couple of Ambien and fell asleep. When I woke up the next morning, it was nearly noon and the house was empty; except for Tory and the housekeeper, everyone else was gone.

CHAPTER
TWENTY-THREE

I did what usually works when my spirits are at ebb—shopping and a massage, with chocolate for a chaser. I ran into Jessie and Zach in the village. They'd been skiing with friends from L.A. who were vacationing at their parents' condo. "We left Rosie with their nanny, we're on our way to pick her up," Jessie said.

"You should have woken me up, I would've taken care of her," I replied. "Where is everyone?"

She shrugged. "Who knows? Evan and Chris were on the mountain, but Alex wasn't with them so we figured he was with you. What did you buy? Is this for Rosie? A little black leather motorcycle jacket? It's so cool, Mom, where did you find it?"

When we got back to the house Alex was there, entertaining a couple of friends from Houston: "Bob and Carol came in on the same plane with Chris and Angela, so I invited them over for drinks," he said.

It was over an hour before they left; they were pleasant enough, but I was glad to see them go. At dinner, Alex drank more than usual; he was sick in the night and it was a long time before he came back to bed.

The next day he was cheerful and affectionate; we didn't talk any more about my "condition," and on the surface, at least, nothing had changed. But in bed it was a different story.

I was accustomed to the rhythms of our lovemaking; I'd learned to savor his slow, unhurried pace, the way he reined in his excitement, holding himself back until I couldn't come one more time before he did. It sounds crass to say it, and I winced when I did (to Carrie, who's the only one I ever share the nitty gritty with) but Alex fucked like a man half his age. Or at least, he had. Now he handled me carefully, as if he was afraid I'd break.

Maybe I wasn't getting his passion, but the mountain seemed to be. He left the house early in the morning, sometimes with the kids, sometimes alone. Paul, who dropped out of college to train for a place on the U.S. Olympic ski team and came within a punishing eight seconds of making it, told me privately that he thought Alex was risking his neck. "I wouldn't even try some of those double black diamonds, not any more," he said dubiously.

I'd been a spectator at Paul's first few important races, but my tension was a distraction: "I can feel it just as I get to the finish line and it throws me off, Mom," he said, so I stopped going. He still skis, but not with the same intensity. One night he said he and Chris had watched Alex from the High Line chair lift that afternoon. "I said, what's with your old man? It's like he's trying to kill himself."

"What did he say?"

"He said his father's always done things his own way, why should he be any different now?"

I tried to bring up the subject with Alex but he brushed me off brusquely. "I don't tell you how to live your life, do I? Don't tell me how to live mine." He apologized later, but his words still stung, especially since I didn't have a comeback.

He was uncharacteristically moody for the rest of the week—sometimes he snapped at his boys, and once or twice at me, especially when I came back in from having my nightly cigarette. Finally I couldn't stand it any longer.

"What's going on?" I asked him.

"What are you talking about?"

"You nearly bit Evan's head off yesterday, just because he left the lights on in the car, and if I were Chris and you talked to me the way you did to him tonight I'd have slugged you."

"Don't tell me how to talk to my kids—I don't tell you how to talk to yours, do I?" he snapped.

"Why? Is there something wrong with the way I talk to them?"

"Besides the fact that you're always telling Jessie what to do with Rosie, and sometimes it seems like you treat Paul more like your lover than your son, no," he said.

"I do not," I said angrily. "At least my kids know I love them."

"And mine don't?"

I threw up my hands. "Alex, stop it. This is crazy. Why are we fighting? I don't know what's going on, but you're not yourself—at least, not the Alex I know."

"Maybe you don't know me as well as you think you do," he said cryptically.

"Maybe I don't," I replied, and he walked out of the room. I tried again the next night. We'd had sex, but it was more cursory than passionate—it felt like a duty fuck, the kind you have when you know you should but don't really want to. Afterward, just as he was turning over to go to sleep, I said, "Alex? Is this because of what I told you?"

"What did you tell me?" he said sleepily.

"You know…about my heart thing. My, umm, condition. Is that why you're being so, well, distant?"

He rolled back over and faced me. "We weren't so distant a few minutes ago, were we?" he said.

"Not physically. But emotionally…you're not here, Alex. I don't know where you are, but you're not with me."

He kissed me on the forehead. "It's not about you, Sugar," he said, more tenderly than he'd spoken in the past couple of days. "It's not

always about you." And then he turned over again, and in minutes
he was snoring.

I had too much on my mind to sleep and I didn't feel like reading or
watching TV, so I went downstairs to what was a decorator's idea of a library,
even though most of the books that lined the shelves didn't look like their
spines had ever been cracked. But there was a desk equipped with a fax
machine, copier, printer and computer. I opened a blank word document
and looked at all that white space for a few minutes and then I began to
outline an idea for a story, which turned into some scenes and then into the
first act of a script for the show.

It was almost dawn when I stopped. That's the thing about writing—
when it's going well, your mind is too occupied to think about anything else.
You don't notice time passing—it's as if you participate in it, a state the
Greeks call *kairos*. You're in a whole other world, one where you make things
happen instead of letting them happen to you. It's always been my escape
hatch, and that night, I was grateful for it. When I printed out the pages later
that day, I was glad to see they were pretty good; by the time New Year's Eve
day rolled around, I had a complete script, or at least a solid draft of one.

By then Alex seemed to have snapped out of his bad mood. He skied
that day, and when he came back to the house he kissed me warmly and said
he thought he'd lie down for a while before the night's festivities began.

Vail pulls out all the stops on New Year's Eve with a big torchlight
parade and fireworks; in addition, Alex and I had accepted invitations to two
parties. One was being hosted by Bob and Carol Hollister, who'd reserved
the Wildflower Restaurant at the Vail Lodge for a private dinner; Hedley
Sturgis, who'd championed my pilot and was still taking a proprietary
interest in the series even though she wasn't directly involved anymore, was
having the other one.

She'd phoned a few days before I left, wanting to nail down a time to
get together after New Year's. She said she'd be in L.A. after the holidays,
which she was spending in Vail with her current girlfriend.

"What a coincidence, I'll be in Vail, too," I said.

"Then you've got to come to our party. Everyone will be there. I'll email you the address."

I was and wasn't looking forward to the party. There was something in Hedley's tone when she called that made me wonder if she had anything else on her agenda besides catching up with an old friend who happened to be producing a new series on her network. I felt a little uneasy when I hung up the phone, and in my Filofax I circled the time and date of our meeting after the holidays with a big red question mark.

It was around seven when Paul tapped softly on our door. Alex was still asleep, and I was editing the draft of the script in the wing chair by the fireplace.

"Are you okay?" he asked.

"I'm fine," I said, closing the door behind me so we wouldn't wake Alex.

"Are you sure?"

"Sure I'm sure. What's the matter?"

"I don't know. I thought maybe you had a migraine, it feels that way."

"No, I don't...are you sure it's me?"

"If it's not Jessie and it's not you ...it might be Alex, Mom. In fact, I'm pretty certain it is. Maybe Kelley ought to take a look at him, she's a nurse— oh, hi, Alex, didn't mean to wake you."

"That's okay, I was just sleeping off a headache—don't look so worried, Sugar, it's nothing, I probably shouldn't have taken that last run today. A couple of aspirin and I'll be fine."

"Are you sure aspirin's all you need, Alex?" Paul shot me a worried look.

"It usually does the trick," he said. "I'm going to take a shower and climb into my monkey suit now, okay?"

"If you really want to," I said. "We don't have to go out if you're not feeling well. Bob and Carol probably won't even notice if we're not there, and I don't care about Hedley's party, I'm seeing her next week anyway."

"What, and miss showing you off in that dress that's hanging on the closet door? Not a chance," he answered.

The dress was a vintage black silk and velvet sheath with jet-trimmed lace sleeves and hardly any back at all. I found it at The Way We Wore, one of my favorite stores; it was an Edith Head original worn by Shelley Winters when she was just cushy, not fat, playing a New York madam in a truly trashy melodrama called *A House is Not a Home*. I'd brought a short white mink jacket from the forties that I picked up a long time ago in a thrift store in Palm Beach—they'd be perfect together

Alex was out of the shower and dressed before I was. He kissed my neck as I fastened the emerald earrings and finished my make-up; in the mirror his face looked flushed, feverish and unwell above his pleated tuxedo shirt.

"Are you coming down with something?" I turned around and touched my lips to his forehead the way I did with the children when they were little.

"A little cold, maybe," he said. "Nothing to worry about. You look beautiful."

I felt that way—it was New Year's Eve, a night that has its own particular resonance for a woman, so I took him at his word, even if I didn't quite believe it, and off we went.

The party was in full swing when we got there —waiters were passing hors d'oeuvres and champagne flutes, and the air was perfumed with expensive scents. Alex steered me through the crowd, stopping now and then to greet old friends: "Hey, Mac, what are you doing here?" he said to a portly man in his seventies who was carrying two glasses and looking around like he'd misplaced someone. "Last I heard, you and Jeannie were halfway around the world on your boat."

"Didn't make it past the Marquesas," he said. "Jeannie got sick, we came home. Ah, there you are, honey, come meet my old friend Alex Carroll, used to play ball for me." A pretty woman half his age flashed us a beauty-queen smile. "Pleased to make your acquaintance," she twinkled.

"My wife, Jennifer," he said. "Read about your company in the *Journal*, "he told Alex." Deal must be just about done, huh?"

"Close of business yesterday," Alex replied.

"Guess you're a free man then. Or maybe not," he added, looking me over like he was judging a brood mare at a horse auction.

""This is my friend Sugar Kane," Alex said. "Sugar, Mac McKinnon. He had a piece of the team, back in the day."

"Still do," he said pleasantly. "Sugar, huh? Used to know a Sugar, she was a TriDelt at SMU. You a Texas gal, Sugar?"

I was saved from declaring my Yankee roots by Carol Hollister, who swooped down on us like a bird of prey. "I'm so glad you made it—we were beginning to wonder if you'd show up, weren't we, Bob? That dress is fabulous, Sugar, wherever did you find it? I'm so glad the boys could come—I've put you all at the same table."

"It was nice of you to invite them," said Alex politely.

"Well, we're all practically family, aren't we? We used to have such good times back in the old days, the Hollisters and the Carrolls, the fearless foursome, didn't we?" she said, kissing him a little too enthusiastically if you ask me, which no one did.

When the arrival of other guests claimed her attention we made our way through the crowd to the napery-draped tables that were set with gleaming silver and crystal, vases of bluebonnets and miniature white roses, and calligraphed place cards affixed to small ceramic replicas of the Texas state flag. Evan and Chris were already there with their girls, who bloomed with the beauty of youth and the promise of new life.

More Texas friends stopped at our table to say hello—Alex stood up and introduced me, but the fourth or fifth time he remained in his chair. Eventually everyone found their tables and took their seats, and the waiters served the first course, fragrant oyster bisque.

Alex barely touched his, and he only took a few bites of his Cornish game hen before he pushed his plate away.

"Are you okay?" I asked quietly. Despite the crowd in the room, the air was well conditioned, but there were beads of sweat on his forehead. "I'm fine," he said. "Stomach's a little queasy, that's all. I'll be right back."

"Is something the matter with Dad?" Evan asked after Alex left the table.

"I think the soup was too rich for his blood," I said, and Chris and Angela exchanged one of those looks only married people give each other, the kind that say things they don't want other people to hear.

It seemed like a long time before Alex returned; dessert had already been served. When he lifted his water glass, I noticed the tremor in his hand.

We didn't linger long after dinner, and when we got back into the car, I asked Alex again if he was all right.

"I'm fine," he said.

"Really? Because frankly, sweetheart, you don't look it."

"I'm okay," he said. "It was a little close in there. I just needed some fresh air."

"Maybe, but I think one party's enough for tonight. I hate all that *auld lang syne* business, those little twisty noisemakers that go off in your face and all the drunks who slobber all over you at midnight. I'd rather be with you. Let's just go home."

"What? And miss my chance to meet the guys from *Queer Eye*?"

His tone was light, but I didn't believe him. There were only pinpricks of light in his eyes—they were as dilated as those of the anorexic English supermodel I'd just seen doing a line of coke in the ladies' room at the Lodge. And he was panting for air, the way I did that night in New York when I went to the hospital. Whatever this was, it was more than a little cold. "Take us back to the house," I told the driver, and when Alex didn't protest, I was sure it was something serious. "No, wait," I said, "is there a hospital near here? Take us there. And hurry, please!"

Alex shook his head weakly. "No, no. Don't listen to her, Joe, the house will be fine." He leaned back against the seat and closed his eyes, mumbling something I couldn't quite hear.

"What did you say?" I asked.

"I said, forget the hospital," he repeated. "They can't fix what's wrong with me."

By the time we arrived at the house he seemed better—at least his breathing was steadier and his color more normal, although he leaned heavily on Joe and me until we got him inside. We led him to a couch and helped him down onto it—"Thanks, Joe, I'm okay, probably had a little too much to drink, you can go now," he said.

He pulled off his black tie and mopped his face with it. "Damn thing was strangling me," he said. "Would you mind getting me a glass of water, darlin'?"

I stood over him while he drained it. "More?" I asked, and he shook his head. He patted the sofa cushion. "Come sit by me," he said.

"What did you mean, nothing wrong they can fix?" I asked. "Alex, something's the matter with you—are you going to tell me what it is or do I have to drag it out of you?"

He stroked my face and let out a deep sigh. Then he said, "I have an aneurysm in my brain."

I was stunned. "How long has it been there?"

"There's no way to know that."

"Has this happened to you before?"

He nodded. "A few times. That day I met you, at the hospital? UCLA Medical Center has one of the best neuroimaging departments in the country. I'd had a couple of scans in Seattle before that but they didn't show anything, and when I started having symptoms again, I was referred there."

"What did they tell you?"

"They looked at the tests I'd had done and then they did some more. They thought there was something there, but they still weren't sure—they said if there was a bubble in my brain it was a small one, and it was pretty stable. And by the time I saw them, I wasn't having any more symptoms. Then when I came down in November—well, you saw how I was then. So I went back to UCLA before I went home. They did some more tests and scans. By then, it was big enough to see."

"Can they operate?"

"It's not in an easy place to reach. Surgically, there's substantial risk involved."

"How much risk?"

"Too much," he said flatly, which really disturbed me—Alex was a man who took risks even when he didn't have to.

"What if it ruptures?"

"The odds are about the same as if they operate, pretty bad...sweetheart, don't cry. It's possible it's been there for years—when I was playing ball, I used to get headaches sometimes, the way I do now, and that was over thirty years ago. It's entirely possible it won't get any bigger than it already is."

"And if it does?"

He shrugged. "It could rupture. And if it ruptures I could die. Or I could have the surgery and still die. Or worse."

I didn't have to ask what could be worse than dying. "Why didn't you tell me?"

"Probably for the same reasons you didn't tell me," he said.

"But that's not the same thing," I began, and he shook his head.

"Close enough," he said. "Maybe not medically, but for, you know, the other reasons."

Just then, the grandfather clock in the foyer began to toll. "Everyone lives on borrowed time, Sugar," Alex said. "You, me, our kids—everybody."

"Yes, but—"He put a finger to my lips, keeping it there until the last second of the old year tolled away. Then he kissed me gently. "Let's not waste any of it."

CHAPTER
TWENTY-FOUR

We went to sleep in each other's arms—I lay awake for a long time with my head on Alex's chest, listening to him breathe, feeling the reassuringly steady beat of his heart. When I woke up he was standing over me with a tray, looking so vital, so full of energy that I thought I'd dreamed the whole thing, the way you do the morning after something terrible happens just before reality rolls over you like a giant wave.

"Breakfast in bed? What's the occasion?"

"Maybe your mother was right. Just don't expect me to make a habit of this—it'll probably be next New Year's Day before I do it again."

"I hope so—you burnt the toast."

"Exactly," he said with a grin, and I couldn't help laughing. If that was the way he wanted to play it, I'd go along. *I don't tell you how to live your life, don't tell me how to live mine.*

The previous night's snow had turned to freezing rain—whether by chance or intention, we all spent the last day and evening together. The men watched football while we packed up and picked up: As Jessie said, wiping the gummy remnants of a teething biscuit off the back of an upholstered chair, "Even I wouldn't rent my house to ten people, a baby, and an incontinent dog for a week." The staff would come in after we left and do the thorough cleaning, but they'd left us well-provisioned with cold-cuts and sandwiches; Zach put a pot of chili on to simmer the day away, and we ate it that night with hot crusty garlic bread salad, and chocolate brownies.

I kept an eye on Alex as unobtrusively as I could. I didn't want him to think I was hovering over him. For now, anyway, I would take my cue from him. I wouldn't say I was in total denial about what he'd told me, but for most of the day I was fine, except when I took a load of Rosie's freshly laundered clothes out of the dryer; I buried my face in her clean, soft undershirts, remembering the day she was born, when I met Alex—"*all the beginnings, the possibilities.*" That was when it hit me all over again.

Paul found me there in the laundry room. "I've been talking to Alex," he said. "Rough deal."

"It's not fair!" I sobbed, burying my head in his chest for comforting.

"No, it's not," he agreed, continuing to hold me until I stopped crying. Wiping my face with one of Rosie's little wash clothes, he said, "Are you going to be okay?"

"Is he?"

"For now. Nobody knows how long. But remember what you told us? You could fall and break your neck, that's no reason to stop walking. You and Alex are a lot alike that way."

One other thing of note happened that day. When I was taking my clothes from the closet to pack them, I accidentally knocked Alex's tuxedo jacket off its hanger. When I picked it up off the floor, something fell out of the pocket. I bent to retrieve it; it was a small blue Tiffany box, smaller than the one my emerald earrings came in. I fingered the box for a few minutes, turning it over and over in my hands without opening it. Then I replaced it in his pocket, finished my packing, and went downstairs for supper.

The next morning after breakfast I said, "Alex, we need to talk."

"Four of my least favorite words in the English language," he said. "What's on your mind, darlin'?"

"You know what's on my mind."

"No, as a matter of fact, I don't. But I'm sure you'll tell me," he replied, not unkindly.

"It's about your...condition."

"Now I'm the one with a condition, huh?"

"Why won't you have the surgery?"

"I told you why. They could cut a big chunk of what makes me a person instead of a vegetable away—at least some of it. I could lose the ability to see, to talk, to think. I could forget who I am, and not know who anybody else is, either. You, for instance."

"But maybe that wouldn't happen. Maybe you'd be okay."

"But what if I wasn't?" He sighed. "Remember what you said about Tory? That as long as she wasn't suffering, you couldn't put her down? Well, if I'm suffering—if they do the surgery and I'm not only not any better, I'm a whole lot worse –who's going to put me down?"

I didn't have an answer for that, so I didn't say anything. After a minute or two he took my hands, one at a time, and kissed my fingertips the way he did before we made love for the first time. "You said something else, too—you said, until then, every day is a gift. Well, every day I wake up in the morning and I've still got all my marbles is a gift." He let go of my hand then. "You'd better get the kids...it's almost time to leave for the airport."

CHAPTER
TWENTY-FIVE

I sank into the empty silence of my house with a groan of relief. When you've lived by yourself for a long time, you don't appreciate how exhausting other people can be. Being alone again felt like it does when you take your hair out of the ponytail it's been in all day and realize you've had a headache for hours.

I didn't appreciate the joys of solitude after the kids were grown and gone and so was the last major man in my life. For a long time after that it was indistinguishable from loneliness. Finally accepting the fact that I'd probably live out the rest of my days and nights as a single woman, after a string of other losses and disappointments, was the tipping point—I fell into a dark, deep pit, worse than the one that followed after Ted left. Then I went into therapy; the second time I went on Prozac, which was cheaper and faster.

What Prozac did was help me pretend to the rest of the world that I was okay until things turned around as they eventually do and I was. The drug seemed to mobilize my intolerance for wallowing in misery, which, according to Peggy, comes from being afraid I inherited the bipolar gene like my sister Joan, and letting the dogs out—giving free rein to my feelings, particularly the bad ones—will set it off. What dwindled away with my depression was also my libido, or at least those occasional flurries of anticipation over a new man; a blind date, a chance encounter, an introduction at a party or event—even, once, at a funeral. Not that most of them in recent years had ever panned out, although sometimes the flurry melted into a pleasant, platonic friendship with a fellow I could call on when an escort was *de rigueur*. One of the mixed blessings of life as a single woman of a certain age is that usually that's not a requirement, the way it was back when, as Gloria used to say, it wasn't the man himself that mattered—any man would do.

Moving to New York finished what the Prozac started. I coasted on the city's energy and possibilities until my career and social life picked up enough for me to generate my own. It helped that in Manhattan, unlike L.A., women aren't self-conscious about being seen in public, especially at night, without a man. Still, going solo on New Year's Eve is bittersweet no matter how old a woman is, which was why I'd been so excited about making an entrance at Hedley's party with Alex on my arm.

I didn't yearn for intimacy the way I once had—not the kind where you get so wrapped up in somebody else's life you lose touch with your own. But by the time I returned to California after being with Alex for a week, I realized it was already too late.

The memory of Alex kissing my neck as I dressed for the New Year's Eve party stabbed me like a paper cut. For the rest of the weekend I tried to distract myself from obsessing about him, but it was like trying to ignore the cheesecake in the freezer. I replayed every moment of our brief affair, every conversation, wondering why he hadn't told me about his condition or worrying that I'd missed the hints that in hindsight seemed obvious—Alex's sudden fatigue when we rode our bikes back to his cabin, what he said about how long it takes to make good wine, how his sons seemed to know a secret about him that I didn't. When those things were too painful to think about, I gave in to some romantic fantasy like choosing the menu for our wedding brunch or imagining us in Paris on our honeymoon. My thoughts and emotions were all mixed up, but one thing was clear: I was incredibly angry at Alex for not telling me what was wrong with him in time to stop me from falling in love with him.

Remember what it's like when you're young and in love, how the future stretches out in front of you, boundless and beautiful? If it happens when you're older you know it doesn't go on forever, and when the end comes it won't be pretty, but you still manage to kid yourself that it's still a long way off. Until it isn't, and you can't, and you have to blame somebody. I blamed Alex. Not just for making me fall in love with him or even face the truth about myself—that I was mortal, too. I was also thoroughly pissed at him for exposing my highly evolved stance on growing old alone for the duplicitous sham it is (even though I know it's still better than being married to the wrong person, and most of the time, it's the way I like it.)

What would I do if, like Alex, I had a time bomb ticking away in my own head? All I'd had was an octopus in my heart, which had disappeared just like the one I came face to face with under water. It might still be hiding inside, biding its time, but it wasn't threatening me right now the way Alex's aneurysm was.

Dying changes everything, but if you're as good at denial as I am, only coming close doesn't. My brush with the octopus hadn't made me work less or smell the flowers more. But for a realist like Alex, who understood exactly what was happening to him, denial wasn't an option: He knew he was going to die very shortly. Unless, of course, he risked something worse before that happened.

Suddenly something went *ka-ching*! in my head the way it does when a piece of the puzzle falls into place, an insight so clear it's undeniable. It wasn't just himself Alex thought he might lose to the bubble in his brain, whether or not he had the surgery –if he told me, he might lose me, too.

Fuck you, Alex Carroll, I thought—*at least I took a risk! Not as big as the one you'll be taking if you let them cut into your brain, but a risk all the same!*

That's what happens when you let someone into your inner world— you take the chance it'll be changed. That's what loving someone is. But if

Alex couldn't open up to me and risk that changing his mind, we didn't even have a limited future together, much less a longer one.

"Not everything's about you, Sugar," he'd said, and while that's often true, I knew this time it wasn't the whole story; he didn't trust me to be able to deal with the reality of his condition, just like I didn't think he could handle mine. There went that *ka-ching* again as I realized why he'd gotten so pissed off when I finally told him what happened to me in Seattle.

Insight is great, but it doesn't mean anything unless you follow it up with action. And as I was pondering what that might be, the rest of my life—the work part—reared its suddenly very ugly head.

CHAPTER
TWENTY-SIX

The readout on my cell showed four calls from Sandro, most recently that morning while I was in the shower, so I phoned him on my way to the studio the first day back after the break.

He didn't even bother with 'Happy New Year.' "Where the hell have you been?" he wanted to know.

I wasn't thrilled by his tone of voice—I wasn't crazy about going back to work, either, but at least it would force me to stop angsting over Alex and the unsettled nature of our relationship.

Except for the script I started writing that night in Vail when I was too wound up to sleep, I hadn't thought about my job since we wrapped for the holiday. In the last few days I'd told my best friends about what was wrong with Alex—I wrapped their sadness for him and empathy for me around me like a hand-knit shawl. They didn't offer me advice, just comfort, which was what I needed.

Alex had called me the night before. He sounded stronger and more like himself but our brief conversation felt as cursory as an air kiss, a meaningless brush of lips in the vague vicinity of someone's cheek. We avoided discussing the elephant in the room; I didn't ask how he was feeling, he didn't volunteer, and neither of us brought up what happened in Vail. "I'm staying in town until the transition's finished," he told me. "Helping the new team settle in and making sure the folks who are leaving are taken care of."

"How long do you think that will take?"

"A few weeks, and then I'm good to go."

"Go where?"

"The island, probably. I'll let you know."

The unspoken message—the one I heard—was that I shouldn't expect to hear from him for a while. "I'm going to be really busy for a while too," I said.

"We'll stay in touch." It wasn't exactly a question, but I answered it anyway.

"Of course we will."

After the phone call I got extremely stoned while listening to a mix tape called *Opus 50* that a friend made for me ten years ago—rueful wisdom about life and love from Joni Mitchell, Bonnie Raitt and Nina Simone, among others. While it was playing the second time I ate a pint of chocolate chunk ice cream. Then I took a bath and cried myself to sleep.

By the next morning I wasn't in the best of all moods and Sandro's hissy fit didn't help. "On vacation, like everyone else. What was so important it couldn't wait?" I said.

"They want to replace you, Sugar," he replied. "And since it's my job to look after your career, I thought you might want to know that before you showed up today. If you showed up."

"Replace me? Are you serious? And what do you mean, if I showed up? Why wouldn't I?"

"Why indeed? That's the question," he said. "Apparently, you haven't been. Not every day, anyway. And when you do, you come in late and leave early."

"Says who?"

"Nelly, the network, the production company. They think you're doing a half-assed job."

"What are they smoking? I've practically been sleeping, eating and breathing that job! I've risked my *life* for that fucking job! If you even knew—"

"All I know is what they're saying, sweetheart," said Sandro more gently. "That you didn't go on all the locations. You miss meetings. You've been sleeping in your office in the middle of the day."

"They didn't need me on those locations, they were mostly shooting exteriors. When I don't come in it's because I'm working at home—I write better away from the office. I even wrote a script last week while I was on my fucking vacation—what about that? And I'm not sleeping when I'm on the couch in my office, I'm thinking!"

"Maybe so," he went on, "but the network's picking up the show for next season. They'll make the announcement at the end of the month. Meanwhile, they're not sure you can finish this one."

"But I have a contract. They can't do that, can they?"

"Sure they can. They might have to pay you but they don't have to play you. Especially when they've got a replacement all lined up."

"Robin." It wasn't a question, and he didn't answer it. "Don't get your tits in an uproar," he said. "We've been talking. I convinced them you were just tired, all you needed was a little vacation. They're willing to guarantee you the rest of this season under certain conditions. You can still turn it around, Sugar, but you'll have to work your *toochus* off to keep them from taking the show away from you."

"What happens if they do?"

"Oh, you'll still make out okay. You'll get development credit as long as the series runs. There'll be dough from repeats, residuals, foreign sales. And you'll get paid as an executive producer until the hiatus in April whether you run the show or not. Not as much as if they have to ante up for Robin or someone else to keep things going while they're still paying you off, but it's not chopped liver, either. So you better decide what you're going to do before you go in there, or they'll tell you."

"Those conditions you mentioned—exactly what are we talking about here? Do I have to punch in and out like I'm on a clock? Am I supposed to report to somebody every time I take a pee? Do they want me to keep a daily log or kiss some asses I might have overlooked, seeing as I've been getting a show on the air and building the ratings?"

Sandro ignored my questions. "They're worried about the season finale. They haven't even seen an outline yet. They want a big close."

"They always want a big close. I'll think one up and give it to them by the end of the week."

"They want something different for next season, so the finale needs to set it up."

"Different how?"

"You know what, Sugar?" said Sandro. "Maybe you should just forget about that one now. We can talk about it in a few days. In the meantime, why don't you concentrate on showing them you've still got what it takes?"

"You think I don't?"

"It doesn't matter what I—" he began, and then I heard a click followed by dead air that means the other person either disconnected or lost your signal. Since I still had plenty of bars, maybe he just didn't want to answer my question.

I couldn't let them fire me in the middle of a season. If you're really big in the business with a string of hits behind you, you can do time, rehab or whatever else is required to pull your shit together and still get work, especially if you're Aaron Sorkin and the suits think they can wring another hit out of you. *But not if you're Sugar Kane, not if they're already worried about whether you can still deliver.*

Flashing what I hoped was a peppy, confident smile at the gate guard, I drove onto the lot. I kept the same smile pasted on my face until I left ten excruciatingly long hours later, and that's how it went for the next several weeks. I arrived at the office before anyone else showed up and was usually the last one to leave. I finished the script I'd started in Vail and told the writers what I wanted done about those we needed for the rest of the season. I went to every single meeting, including the low-level ones I'd sent Robin to until now—casting, locations, budgets, publicity, even catering. And I didn't indicate to anyone at all that my job was in jeopardy. "Be smart about playing dumb," Sandro had suggested. "Let them think you don't know anything."

"That's easy, I don't. Until they announce we're being picked up, I can't hang on to my writers. My best one is leaving to work for that new show about the serial killer with the heart of gold. What are they waiting for?"

"Have they said anything to you about the last show yet?"

"No, but that's not unusual. The don't ordinarily see a script until I give them a final draft."

The day after I told Sandro that, Robin stuck her head in my office. "We have a meeting with Patrick and Claudia at Nelly's tomorrow at ten. It's about the finale."

"Good," I said absentmindedly. "I'm working on it now. It'll be finished by then."

"Really?" she asked. "I didn't realize you'd already started on it." You know how some people can make their voices sound snide and skeptical at the same time, while others merely raise an eyebrow? Robin does both. "I'd be glad to look it over if you think it needs another pair of eyes," she said.

"Thanks, but I think I've got it covered."

I didn't, quite, but I would by the next morning, even if I had to stay up all night to do it.

On the way home from the office I stopped at a takeout place for dinner—I hadn't been shopping for real groceries or cooking them since Sandro goosed my work ethic into overdrive after the holiday break.

It was dark when I turned into my driveway. Usually Tory hears me arrive and meets me just inside the front door, her tail thumping in welcome.

Since she didn't come when I called her, I flicked on the lights in the back yard to see if she'd gone outside through the pet door in the kitchen and was absorbed in some doggy pleasure like digging up a bone or treeing a squirrel. There's still plenty of local wildlife wandering around even in the residentially cultivated parts of the Canyon; although I wasn't really worried about Tory getting eaten by a coyote, I made an uneasy foray around the property before I gave up and went back inside. *She'll come home when she's ready—she's probably pissed off because I've left her alone so much lately.*

I heard and smelled her before I found her. First there was a kind of keening moan—not exactly like a baby's cry, but human enough to startle me. I traced it up the stairs, not finding Tory right away but following the unmistakable odor of shit into my bedroom and getting down on my hand and knees next to the bed. She was hiding under it, quivering in embarrassment over losing control of her bowels. But what was worse was the way she shied away from my touch when I reached under the bed to pet her.

"It's okay, baby, you just had a little accident," I crooned soothingly. I couldn't gentle her out, so finally I squirmed under the bed and pulled her out by her collar.

She made a couple of efforts to stand up, but her back half seemed lifeless—she couldn't straighten out her rear legs or even her tail, and after she tried and failed she made that keening sound again. I picked her up and sat down on the bed with her in my lap; she peed a few drops, and then fell into a stupor.

Ignoring the wetness on my thighs, I petted and stroked her and talked to her. I said I was sorry I'd left her alone so much lately. I told her I loved her as much as the world and more. I promised that as soon as we got to the vet she'd be fine. Maybe it was just a coincidence—she hates the word 'vet'—but as soon as I said it I felt her tail wag against my knees, and then she lifted her head up and licked my face.

When I lowered her to the floor, she stood up, took a couple of wobbly steps and walked out of the bedroom to the top of the stairs, looking back twice to make sure I was following her. I exhaled a breath I wasn't aware of holding and we went downstairs together.

The vet was closed and I didn't want to take her to the Valley to the emergency clinic, especially since that night she seemed to be her old self again, eating her regular diner, relieving herself outside the way she always did, and moving around easily. She stretched out at my feet under my desk and I finished a complete treatment for the season finale. Then I e-mailed it to Nelly so she could look it over before our meeting the next day and Tory and I turned in.

I fell asleep right away; I was too tired to think but not to dream, and when Tory made that awful keening noise early the next morning I thought it was being made by the baby Alex was holding out to me—the baby from the hospital nursery that looked like Condoleeza Rice.

I'd been pretty good about keeping Alex walled off in a small corner of my mind the last few weeks; I couldn't afford to dwell on anything but the show. He e-mailed me that he'd finished his business in Seattle and was going up to his cabin in the islands, and called a couple of times after that.

"I need to be alone for a few days and decide what I'm going to do next," he said.

"Are you reconsidering the surgery?"

"I'm reconsidering everything," he told me, and if there was an opening there, I didn't take it. Instead, I worked harder than I had in years: It was my show, and nobody, not even Robin, was going to take it away from me.

When Tory cried I woke up, but then she licked my face and bumped my head with her muzzle, a sign that she needed to go out. She fell rather than jumped off the bed but she managed to make it downstairs all the way through the hall and the dining room until she collapsed suddenly a few feet from the doggy door in the kitchen. As her urine puddled around her, she hung her head in shame.

She didn't get up again under her own power. After I watched her valiant attempts and listened to her pitiful whimpers for a few minutes, I threw on some clothes, wrapped her in a blanket and drove to the vet in Westwood. The receptionist said the schedule was full until 11:30: "We'll wait," I said, but when Tory moaned a few more times she left the front desk; when she came back, she said the doctor would see us next even though I hadn't called ahead to tell them it was urgent.

I would have, but my cell phone was still where I'd left it in its charger on the counter. Instead, I used that seemingly endless time in morning traffic praying, pleading and bargaining with god for Tory to be okay.

The vet took a long time examining Tory, listening to her heart and lungs, palpating her belly, and tapping her legs with a reflex hammer. The front legs twitched, the back ones didn't react, and when the vet inserted a rectal thermometer, Tory didn't seem to notice.

When she finished, she put Tory in my lap. Then she went to the sink and washed and dried her hands before turning to me. "I think it might be time to put her down," she said, briskly but not unfeelingly. "The paralysis is intermittent now, but soon it will be permanent. She can't control her bladder or bowels. I can give you something for her discomfort, but she won't have a very good quality of life. At least, not one you'd want for anyone you loved."

I couldn't make that choice for Alex and I wasn't sure I could make it for Tory, either. "It's natural to try to keep them alive as long as possible," the vet continued. "But we have to think about whose sake it's for."

I didn't want to listen; instead, I buried my face in Tory's fur, fighting back my tears helplessly until they dripped on her coat and she twisted her head around to peer at me in confusion. Finally I pulled myself together. "Is there any sense in waiting?" I asked. "Any chance she could get better?"

The vet shook her head. "Not really. All we can do is make the pain easier to bear."

"Then let's do it."

She left the room for a few minutes; when she returned she was carrying a syringe and a plastic sheet, which she spread out on my lap and then placed Tory gently down on it. I scrunched my face down next to hers and nuzzled her, mouthing made-up sounds—booja booja, kiss kiss, good doggy. Seconds after the vet slipped in the needle Tory licked me again; her tongue left a damp trail on my cheek when she stopped moving.

"Do you want to stay here with her for a while?" asked the doctor after she listened for a heartbeat and put her stethoscope away.

"Maybe a few minutes," I replied, but as soon as she was gone Tory's lack of life, her absence even though she was still lying in my lap, sunk in. I felt it in her body first and then in mine, and suddenly I had to get out of that airless room.

I wrapped Tory up and left her there on the chair. Then I went back to the front desk.

"Unless you object, we'll have her cremated," the veterinary assistant told me, expressing her sympathy for my loss. "We can make the arrangements and return the ashes to you unless you want us to dispose of them. Shall we call you when they're ready?"

I agreed, and signed the consent form. By the time I left Westwood it was almost noon. I'd missed the meeting with Nelly and the others but I didn't really care. I couldn't think of one good reason not to go home, crawl into bed, and miss my best friend.

CHAPTER
TWENTY-SEVEN

When I came in the next day my desk was littered with pink message slips from Nelly, the production company suits, Robin and Sandro. I ignored them all; instead I wrote them a group e-mail explaining my absence at the meeting. I attached another copy of the treatment for Nelly in case she hadn't already read it and after I pushed "send" I closed my office door and put my head down on my desk.

Nelly's response wasn't long in coming. "It's very nice, but as you'd know if you'd been at the meeting we've decided to go in a different direction next season, and since this doesn't set that up, we can't use it," she said when she called.

"What direction is that?" I asked, but she was vague in her reply.

"Oh, a few cast changes, a shift in the emphasis on certain people," she said. "We've done a few focus groups and, well...Look, why don't I just send you the memo about what we decided, and Robin's outline?"

Robin's outline? For the finale? Where the fuck had I been while they were doing their focus groups, making their decisions, and writing their memos?

"You do that," I said, more politely than I felt. By the time I left the office, the outline hadn't arrived, and Robin hadn't come in either.

Almost as if they'd timed it (the notion that you're under surveillance isn't restricted to paranoiacs), my computer zinged with the bell of arriving email a few minutes after I got home. I sat down at my desk to read it. Then I went for a long swim in the pool next door and when I came home I read it again.

The long and short of it was that they were getting rid of Amelia and refocusing the show around Clea and her on-again, off-again romance with the boyfriend we'd had to replace in the pilot. In the finale they wanted both mother and daughter kidnapped and Amelia killed off, perhaps by an accidental discharge from the boyfriend's gun when he breaks in to rescue them. The set-up for the second season was Clea trying to keep the agency solvent, at the same time playing I love him/I hate him, on again off again, with the young man who killed her mother.

The memo discussed demographics, target audiences, "Q" scores and a few comments from the focus groups referencing Amelia—"She's like the mother from hell, why doesn't Clea stand up to her more?" was one, and another said Amelia was the only thing wrong with the show.

I'd only swum up one not-very-good response to what was being proposed, a version of what I'd been so unwilling to consider months before when Robin and her erstwhile agent—who was now much more than that, according to office gossip—first suggested it; the tired old ghost chestnut where Amelia is a spectral presence who makes herself visible whenever Clea's in trouble or needs motherly advice. But when I got out of the pool and came home to my Tory-less house, I knew that idea was as dead as my dog.

In the morning I made myself presentable for work, then dawdled over coffee and the newspaper until I couldn't procrastinate any longer. I'd turned the key in the ignition and backed halfway down the driveway before I shifted into drive and put the car back where I always parked it and went back inside, where I wrote Sandro a long e-mail explaining that I had no interest in writing or running the next season the way the network wanted me to or signing off on Robin's outline for the last episode of this one.

Let him do the explaining—that's what I pay him for, as he so often reminded me. I sent the e-mail and turned off my computer. Then I packed enough clothes for a few weeks, turned off my cell phone and stuck it in the glove compartment of the car and headed north.

I spent the first night in a motel in Ashland, Oregon. Late the next afternoon I passed the Seattle exits on I-5 and kept driving for another hour until I reached Anacortes, where I boarded a Washington State ferry for the San Juan Islands. It was raining, a steady downpour that kept most of the passengers in their cars or the cabin. I went outside on the uppermost deck and sat on a bench under heat lamps that glowed redder as dusk turned to evening and the smudgy line between the sea and the darkening sky disappeared.

The weather made the last part of the trip to the cabin slow and difficult; it made me think of that line from E.L. Doctorow, who said writing is like taking a trip at night in your car: You can only see as far as your headlights illuminate, but driving that way you can get all the way home.

There were lights on in Alex's cabin; a couple of minutes after I turned off the engine he came out on the front deck. He knew my car but didn't move toward it; he just stood there until I reached him, all the words I'd rehearsed on the way hanging unspoken in the air between us.

"How long are you here for?" he said finally.

"As long as you want me here. Or forever, if that comes first."

"That could be a pretty short time."

"So? It's like you told Evan—the long shots are the ones worth playing."

"You're going to try to talk me into letting them cut on my brain, aren't you?"

"My father used to say that nagging was the leading cause of death in married men," I said. "That may be true, since he was eating a plate of fried egg and matzo brie while Frances was reminding him about his cholesterol when he keeled over."

"Does that mean you're not going to get on my case?"

"No, it just means I'll try to restrain myself. It's your life, Alex. And every day of it's a gift."

"What if it's our life?"

"If it isn't, what am I doing here?"

He smiled. "I don't know, darlin'—what *are* you doing here?"

"Taking a risk," I said. "After all, what's life worth without risk?"